Forgiven

Forgiven

A
Novel
By
Harry "Buddy" Beckett

Artistic Spaces Publishing

Flemingsburg, KY

Credits:
Poems by Harry "Buddy" Beckett
    "Waiting"
    "Daily Notes"
    "No Sweeter Love"
    "My Dream"
    "Foolish Heart"
Poem by James Henry Leigh Hunt:
    "Abou Ben Adhem"
Song Lyrics by Paul Francis Webster:
    "The Loveliest night of the Year"

Notice: This is a work of fiction. Names, characters, places, and incidents are either products of the author's imagination or, if real, are used ficticiously.

Library of Congress Control Number: 2009913764
Subject Headings
1. Religious Fiction
2. Romance

ISBN 10: 0-9796328-5-4
ISBN 13: 978-0-9796328-5-3

Published by: Artistic Spaces Publishing Company
    P.O. Box 54
    Flemingsburg, KY 41041

Printed in the United States of America

This novel is dedicated to
—readers who pray believing—

Thanks Lois Collins Rimmer for your skill
and insight.

Contents

*And all things, whatsoever ye ask in
prayer, believing, ye shall receive.*
Matthew 21:22 KJV

PROLOGUE

Michael Bentley couldn't remember a drearier day when he arrived at the hospital. Through the window, he had mostly stared at a mouse-gray sky for three days. A year ago just before Christmas, he was in another hospital and somehow survived the loss of his father. In his present distraught state, surviving was not an option this December 2003. He was so regretful. His selfish lust was why his only true love was dying. If he could only step back in time and relive just one yesterday.

His tired and bewildered mind was tumbling without any thought of another hour or another tomorrow. During the day, he watched rain drops make meandering rivulets down the window glass. Each drop was a shared dream sliding from hopeful pursuit. Michael had always been a man of action who could help things happen. He wasn't pushy or arrogant but capable and confident. With some wisdom and some luck, he had accomplished a great deal in his young life.

He remembered last August aboard his sailboat; he had unexpectedly recovered from losing his father. His life took a new happy course that was now ending as he sat with his head in his hands. There would be no more tears, no more prayers and no more hope.

Ten minutes earlier, a stern-faced doctor walked into the room and spoke in a pitiless monotone.

"The patient (Sommer Renée Rose) is experiencing a most severe form of unconsciousness. With this type of coma, the brain has lost the ability to perform vital body functions."

He glanced at the mechanical ventilation device, "Including maintenance of breathing."

The doctor looked out the window before abruptly stating, "Results of extensive testing indicate that the patient is legally . . . " He stopped talking and stared at the patient. Even the disciplined doctor couldn't say dead. He turned and looked at the older woman.

"There is cessation of all brain functions, even though the heart continues to beat."

While Michael was trying to comprehend what he thought he heard, the doctor added, "We are not hopeful. Later today you will need to make a decision concerning the ventilator."

Fourteen months ago, two young people falling in love could have never imagined the spring of life would unwind this way.

Chapter One

Wispy strips of lemon yellow mingled with a dozen shades of red, which highlighted a serene expanse of bubbling purple-clad clouds. This majestic beauty was slowly expanding while being sprinkled with leaven from warm October winds rising from crevices in the east Tennessee hills. The blushing source of this splendor had already slipped below the horizon before Michael Bentley parked his car. He marveled at the heavenly, mottled masterpiece painted on the misty gold-flecked twilight of this Sunday evening.

He had been traveling from Columbus, Ohio since 7 a.m. and was ready for rest. His destination since leaving Asheville, North Carolina was Dandridge, Tennessee and a Comfort Inn. After check-in, he cruised the lakefront road of Douglas Lake a few miles before crossing I-40 onto State Route 92. He traveled thence to US Route 31E to Jefferson City and then to New Market. Michael quickly drove through some streets of Jefferson

City. The little town seemed ready to roll up the sidewalks as daunting and spooky remnants of the recent glorious sunset were painting drab layered shadows on low, mute buildings. The wind was just a whisper tossing some dry colored leaves along empty streets and sidewalks. The only movement Michael saw during his sprint through town was a frazzled dog. It was loping along with its two hind legs noticeably misaligned from the front ones. He always smiled when seeing a dog running "sideways."

He drove to New Market and then straightway back to the motel, checking the distance at a little less than five miles.

Thirty minutes later, after a quick shower, he was propped up in bed. On his little jaunt, he stopped two times in Jefferson City and one time in New Market. Each stop had been at a real estate office. From depositories in front of the offices, he claimed a free copy of local real estate listings offered for sale. He had also scanned real estate listings in Mount Airy and Asheville, North Carolina. He slowly looked at the two booklets from Jefferson City. Repeating the slow review for the New Market listings took a little longer than the other two. On the cover and on page three, he read with interest the description of two large houses, each featuring a beautiful view. Page three was dog-eared. The next to the last page was also marked with a folded-down corner. Michael repeatedly looked at the second marked page.

After a while, the Yankee from Ohio closed his tired eyes. The drive to Tennessee had been most pleasant. The view through the windshield was constantly swarming with splashy colored autumn leaves. But right now, the view in his heart was of another plane—another dimension—beyond the beautiful phenomenon of the sunset.

Michael Bentley reverently bowed his head and prayed aloud.

Dear Lord, thank you for my safe trip today. And above all else dear Lord, thank you for answering my special prayer. It's the one we talked about last August. Now, I'm going to buy Kathleen a surprise wedding present and also help a woman named Sommer receive a nice commission. Thank you Lord for so many blessings. Amen

Michael processed a sharing heart that propelled him to willingly show kindness and to help others less fortunate than him. After looking again at the next to the last page in the New Market real estate booklet, a thankful Yankee in east Tennessee was soon peacefully asleep.

A minute after nine, Michael called the Oxford Realty office.

"Hello, Oxford Realty—Alice speaking. May I help you?"

"Yes, Hi Alice—my name is Michael Bentley, I'd like to speak with Sommer Rose."

"Ooookay. Just a minute— she's here somewhere."

"Alice, before she comes to the phone, could I ask you a question?"

"Why yes of course."

Alice had already decided that she liked the man connected with the voice. Michael's voice was smooth without any indication he was talking down to the receiver. She had only heard a few words but had a feeling of knowing him a long time.

"Does Sommer work full-time?"

"Yes, but why do you ask?

"Well Alice, I noticed in your listings that hers were the lowest value units. So, I thought maybe . . . "

Alice quickly pounced during his lull, "Oh no, she's full time. She's been with us a year. As for her page—well she's . . . well I guess she's . . . " Alice whispered the rest of the sentence, " . . . still learning. Here she comes Mr—"

Michael interrupted, "Wait Alice, maybe she's not suited for selling real estate."

She didn't answer in the allotted time he was willing to wait, so he blurted, "Alice, let me tell you the truth why I'm asking. I'm looking to buy a house and picked Sommer because I thought that maybe she would appreciate the business."

Still no reply from Alice. "Hello, you there?"

"Yes . . . I'm sorry . . . I've been wiping tears. I've been praying that Sommer might . . . well . . . She could use a sell. Yes, a sell would be nice because there's no husband to help."

"Thank you Alice, you have been most helpful. I'm from Ohio, and I'm enjoying the southern hospitality."

Alice, a thirty-five year-old divorcee, was sure she was in love with this nice sounding Yankee.

"Here's Sommer, Mr. Bentley."

"Hello Mr. Bentley, I'm Sommer. How may I help you?"

Sommer's lyrical voice flooded his whole being with a contented happiness. Why this was happening, he wasn't sure. He didn't understand why he couldn't breathe. He didn't count on this.

"Alice, who is this man?"

Michael quickly spoke. "Hi Sommer, I'm Michael."

"Hi Michael, how may I help you?"

"I'm looking for a house with a beautiful view."

Normally Sommer would say something like—"We have two houses with a view." Maybe Sommer connected with the pleasing voice like Alice did, or maybe some inner intensity prompted her reply.

"Michael." She spoke with an inflection as if they were close friends. "We have two houses with a beautiful view. One is outstanding. We print a booklet of our listings and this fantastic house is featured on the front cover. The other one is on page three."

Sommer had delivered her pitch without breathing. But she wasn't finished. "I could show you the houses today if —"

Michael didn't let her complete her statement. "I would like to see them today, Sommer. I can be there in twenty minutes."

"Okay Michael. I'll watch for you."

You may wonder why Michael was experiencing trouble breathing after hearing Sommer voice. This was the second time he had difficulty breathing within the last two months. Let's back up and find out why.

Last December, just before Christmas, he lost his father. He almost died himself. Nothing before had so totally disoriented him. He was bewildered, distracted and finally embarrassed for his conduct. His grandfather's death four years before had impacted his life more than he thought it would, but nothing near the quandary of losing his dad. He dearly loved his dad and missed his parental ascendancy. They were in business together and suddenly he, the young son, was in charge. But that part was not the source of his depression. Michael and his dad had a closeness few fathers and sons enjoy. They were like-minded in many ways, sharing many opinions and conjectures about life from the same perspective. Oh yes, Michael missed his dad more than he knew he should until the following August.

He was in his sailboat when suddenly he completely realized the gravity of his father's death with relation to his remaining days on planet earth. He had a life to continue with a forward look. No more depression—regret yes—but no more cataracts of gloom to dim the bright future beyond each setting sun. He had many new dawns to experience and many new dreams to follow. He had draughts of cheerful tomorrows to drink. He was going to change his thinking so his great void could be relegated to just drops of remembrance.

Later that sunny, August Sunday, his intentions were manifested as his life clearly changed directions. He started trekking a new happy way. His fresh course was not altered by a magnetic bearing but by a divine inspired intervention while reading the Bible. A scripture verse in Matthew became a crux to tack the gloomy winds of depression surrounding him after losing his Dad.

> *And all things, whatsoever ye ask in prayer,*
> *believing, ye shall receive.*
> —*Matthew 21:22 KJV*

After reading the verse several times, an explosive sensation was suddenly all over him. When his jubilant mind cooled from boiling thankfulness, a servile Michael Bentley yielded to a moment of understanding with the Holy Spirit. He humbly bowed and asked Jesus to grant a special prayer request for him as he began his new direction. "Help me Lord to find a girl to partner with me through this earthly life." At that instance, he knew it would be answered because as he asked, he believed.

Two days later, his mother announced that she had arranged for him to meet a girl from a prominent Columbus family (with celebrated wealth). She convinced him he would be glad to meet this beautiful socialite. He had dated five girls, and the three he brought home to meet his mother didn't please her. She always found at least one fault with his choices. Being an obedient son, he agreed to meet Kathleen Eastwood. He was happy when he first saw her and instantly believed she really was the answer to his prayer.

Cupid must have flapped his wings vigorously because Michael Bentley was swept off his feet. Kathleen was even more than he had dreamed. She was agreeable, amiable, warm, and sweet tempered. Michael was out-of-his-mind in love. After being together seventeen times during the first month, Kathleen accepted a large engagement ring. Mother was ecstatic.

The next day, after a pompous, backyard, Labor Day spectacle when the engagement was announced, Kathleen Eastwood began changing from being sweet and submissive to being condescending and dictatorial. The endearing winds that brought them together had reverted to the proverbial whirlwind. During the remaining days of September, they had attended six dinner parties which she had arranged. Michael enjoyed the first three and then realized he was being paraded before her jet-set friends as her latest trophy. He refused to attend the seventh party, telling her his business was being neglected. She pouted as a spoiled child would, but modified her attitude enough to stabilize the engagement. This was not her first acceptance of a pledge to marry. Michael didn't know she had been engaged before. As a matter of fact, she had a small velvet pouch with a gold metallic drawstring that contained four diamond rings she had refused to return to jilted fiancées. But this Michael man was different from her other trophies. Kathleen, the playgirl, was trying to be serious for the first time in her fun-filled leisure life.

Michael worked extended hours at his office during the first few days in October. He and Kathleen talked a lot on the phone and had lunch together two times. He sincerely believed they were becoming a compatible pair. Yet, deep within his conscience, disturbing thoughts would reverberate and periodically surface. To quench his matrimonial doubts and know for sure that Kathleen was the answer to his prayer, he had a plan of action to pursue. He didn't intend to play a game with God but as a precautionary posture he wanted a convincing sign to confirm his lifelong commitment to his betrothed. He was going to take a sabbatical and leave his routine for a short time down south. He repeatedly convinced himself that this was no game with God but a testing of his heart to be sure about the rest of his life with Kathleen. At times, he was ashamed for his doubts because he had already decided to buy her a house for a surprise-wedding gift.

When Michael finished his "memory trip," he couldn't explain why he was so aroused after hearing Sommer's voice.

Chapter Two

Sommer was in John Oxford's office and didn't see a white Lexus parking out front. John, the owner, was telling her that she needed to sell a listing soon or her job would be terminated. Alice saw a young man approach the office with a determined gait. Sommer was standing by her desk when Michael momentarily stopped in the doorway. Both Sommer and Alice saw him at the same time. Both reacted by staring and realizing he was well over six feet tall by referencing the doorway height as a gauge.

Michael, wearing tan Dockers and a dark blue pocket tee, walked straight to Alice extending his hand.

"I'm so happy to meet you Alice. It was such a delight to talk with you on the phone. You are among the group of caring people that make daily living a pleasure."

Alice silently looked at Michael. First, how did he know me from Sommer? And who is this man—a preacher? He had seen Sommer's picture in the listing booklet, and from his phone conversation with Alice, he assumed they were good friends and sat close together.

"Alice thanks again. I already like Tennessee."

Maybe it was the suntan or the sparkling blue eyes slightly inset below a prominent brow that rendered Alice speechless. Michael smiled—again revealing white teeth that were a signal contrast to his sailboat tan. With a nod, he turned from the mute Alice to look at an equally surprised Sommer Rose. She could hardly believe this handsome man was so close to her and would presently speak to her.

"Hi Sommer." Michael said no more as he waited for a reply.

"Hello Mr. Bentley."

"It's Michael."

"Oh, well hello Michael."

Her delivery was not ebullient like their phone conversation. Sommer's voice quivered slightly, as she looked at dense, dark, blonde hair guilty of shallow waves. His eyebrows were arched and heavy. She had diverted her eyes when a constriction was felt in her throat.

"Are we ready to look at houses?"

"Yes."

"Okay, lead the way."

After a step from the desk, Michael turned and said, "Goodbye Alice."

"Goodbye and good luck." Alice didn't know if she was wishing good luck to one of them or both of them.

Michael started toward his car before he realized Sommer was walking the opposite direction.

"Hey Sommer, we'll go in my car."

With a firmness that he knew not to counter, Sommer replied, "I'll drive." Her car was clean but ten or more years old and ornamented with assorted "dings".

Sommer was anxious and inwardly excited to be showing houses, especially these two. But for some reason, Michael's presence was subjugating her zeal to effectively pitch the houses. She would usually state some pertinent facts while driving— Michael interrupted her thoughts.

"So Sommer, where are we heading?"

"Oh I'm sorry, we're going to the cover house—we call it The Zilgler House."

"Could we stop at that restaurant?"

"You need breakfast?"

"No. Coffee."

When parked, Sommer made no move to leave the car.

In his bubbling manner, he said to a somber Sommer, "Come on, let's get some coffee."

"I'll wait."

"I thought we could talk about the house."

With this interjection, her thoughts shifted to commission, and she entered the restaurant.

Michael ordered two cups of black coffee. Sommer looked at him with her head slightly tilted implying—how did you know I drink black coffee? He maintained eye contact until Sommer diverted her eyes to the table. After a moment, she was again looking at Michael. He smiled and said, "Sommer, you seem to be a person who gets to the point and moves on with your endeavors. So I believed you wouldn't take time to put cream and sugar in your coffee. A smile confirmed his thesis.

Sommer didn't want any more coffee but was rather enjoying this cup since it was served with a pleasing view across the table. Michael was thinking the same as they sat without talking. She saw a suntanned face framed with strong jaws that was dripping with masculinity. But it was his charming smile that captivated her interest to learn more about this autumn leaf that blew down from Ohio.

Michael was looking at a stolid person who didn't seem to enjoy any happy emotion or passion; he was disappointed. But he did see a young person who processed uncluttered beauty. Her mostly narrow face had a fair complexion that looked cleansed with only soap and water. Her cheeks were accented with a slight blush that looked natural. There was something below the surface about her that was a bit disturbing. Something within her seemed to inhibit the Sommer he wished her to be.

"Well Sommer, shall we go?"

"What about the house?"

"I thought we were going to go see it."

"But you said we would talk about it . . . "

"Oh so I did. Tell me then—why should I buy this house."

"But you haven't seen it yet."

Sommer appeared to be relaxing as she smiled during her last remark. Michael jumped up and hurried to stand behind Sommer's chair. "Okay! Let's go."

Just before entering the driveway, Michael called out rather loudly, "Wow! Look at that arch. The entrance was indeed impressive. A native stone arch ten feet tall was covered with a vine of bright red leaves. Sommer didn't even slow as they passed under it. Michael called again, "Stop! Back up, please, I want to read the inscription."

Sommer obligingly stopped and backed up until they were parked in front of the archway. The vine and leaves were thick and almost covered all of the engraving on the keystone.

Excitedly Michael said, "See that Sommer? That's the name of this estate. See on the keystone—Serendip. That's the name. She agreed and admitted that she didn't know the estate had a name, and apparently Marci didn't know either.

"Who's Marci?"

"She's the sales associate who listed the property."

"Do you know anything about that name?

"No, should I?"

"Well, maybe not, but have you ever heard the word Serendipity?"

"Yes, I've heard it but can't remember what it means.

"Boy! This is something else. Just think—finding this name is a sign. Do you believe in signs that foretell some event?"

"I don't think so—no not really. What are you talking about?"

"Serendipity is a word coined by an English writer a long time ago. I don't remember his name but it's about a fairytale where three princes of Serendip had a knack for finding good accidentally. See? I found this place by accident. Well, that's not exactly true.

Sommer curiously asked, "What do you mean? You haven't seen it yet."

"Oh yes I have. I've seen a picture."

"Well, so you have. But what about the other—"

Michael put up his hand stopping her in mid-sentence. "I didn't really mean by accident. The Lord led me to it. I may explain later. Let's go see this fairytale house."

Sommer bowed as she glanced in his direction, "As you wish." They both smiled and sat in silence as she drove along the winding driveway lined on both sides with large, white pine trees. The invigorating drive was about the length of a football field.

When stopped, they remained in the car a few seconds before Michael said, "I'll open your door."

"That's okay, I'll do it."

The house, or mansion, was large and impressive. Sommer had parked at the back in front of a three-car garage. The exterior was stone with many windows. Michael guessed by the color that the stone was sandstone. Still without talking, Sommer led the way to the front, passing a large windowed room. Once there, Sommer stopped, but Michael continued walking down the sloping front yard to a flagstone area by a low, stone wall. When he reached the wall, he turned and waved for Sommer to come to him. When she got to the flagstone terrace, Michael was sitting on the wall with his legs on the cliff side.

"Come sit down."

"Oh no, I don't like heights."

"Don't worry, there's a ledge ten feet down that would stop you should you fall. Come on."

Sommer slowly walked to the wall and sat with her legs on the yard side, facing Michael.

"I thought you said this house had a beautiful view."

Disappointedly, Sommer asked, "You don't like this view?"

"This view is much, much more than beautiful—it's, it's exquisite, magnificent, elegant, divine and a dozen more adjectives."

"How 'bout lovely."

"That's one."

Michael was quiet as his eyes feasted on more of nature's beauty than he believed he had ever seen. Far below was a small, rocky stream. Just a calm murmur could be heard as mountain-clean water tumbled over smooth rocks. Thousands of trees were adorned in their finest October colors. Leaves fluttered when an occasional warm air would rise to the hilltops. No other sound was heard except his heart. This was the most peaceful place he had ever been, and this was the happiest day in his life other than the day his heart was filled with the love of Jesus. His mind replayed 'the happiest day in his life' thought and added—since meeting Kathleen.

He turned his buzzing head and looked at Sommer who was looking at him. When he first saw her in the real estate office, he seemed to flip inside. He saw a beautiful and exemplary person who seemed to be encased in a shimmering luster. He believed she could have been an angel, except for her somber countenance—not dismal, but not happy like he envisioned an angel must be. At this moment, as their eyes were fixed on each other, he realized what he couldn't think of in the restaurant—she had a worried appearance. Nevertheless, he had to acknowledge she was still beautiful. He had come south from Ohio with a plan, and now he would tell her his intentions.

"Sommer, have you wondered why I am looking for a house?"

She was absorbed in her own thoughts about this handsome man without a wedding band. She knew he had not just removed it because there was no white area on his suntanned finger.

"What? What about the house?"

"I said have you wondered why I'm looking for a house?"

"Well—" Michael didn't give her a chance to finish.

"I want to buy a house to surprise my fiancée."

Sommer concealed her disappointment well. It wasn't hard, since she was good at camouflaging her unhappiness. So this bit of cheerless news was just another chapter in the saga of her unpleasant life. Sommer's life had indeed been unpleasant and also a life with only bare essentials. Her childhood dreams were still floating somewhere out of reach. When she first saw that Michael didn't have a wedding ring, a glimmer of hope stirred in the compartment of forgotten expectations that warmed her heart. And now, sitting ten feet from him in this tranquil place, she looked away and thought, "He'll never know that I have fallen in love with him." A year or two earlier she would have cried and screamed, "Why is this happening to me?" Sommer was now casehardened and moving onward in life, dodging and deflecting disappointments routinely. She had even become semi-comfortable in her disconsolate valley.

"Now, I need to buy a house."

"Well, we should look inside and . . . "

Michael walked closer to Sommer who was standing looking in the direction of the house. He stepped in front of her and asked, "Do you like this house?"

"Michael." For some reason, Sommer was comfortable repeating his name even knowing he was engaged. "It doesn't matter what I think. I'm here to show this house and do the paper work."

"Okay, show on. But wait, I was asking if you liked the house from a woman's perspective."

Sommer looked at him and answered in a tone that implied any woman would like this house. "Yes, Michael I like this house. I like it very much."

"Good."

Michael was looking at the house and blurted, "I remember— Walpole! Henry Walpole. No—not Henry. Harold? No—not Harold.

"What are you talking about?"

"The author . . . "

Sommer's expression continued a conveyance that she didn't know what he was talking about.

"Ohhh, you know—Serindip."

Michael closed his eyes and lowered his head before shouting, "Horace! That's it. Horace Walpole." He smiled and said, "Let's look inside."

At a little before noon, Michael and Sommer were having lunch together. They had also looked at the other house with a view. It was called the Thompson place listed at $370,000. He had persuaded her to have lunch and help him decide what to do. He really did like both places but was going to buy the

Zilgler House. Of course, Sommer didn't know his intentions at this time. Part of his plan was to learn all he could about Sommer Rose. He was going to be with her a bit longer before signing a contract.

"You know Sommer, I like both houses, but $1,400,000 is a lot more than the Thompson place."

Sommer had been quiet during the meal and didn't answer. After she found out he was engaged, she had only been talking to answer direct questions.

"What should I do?"

"Do?" She answered quickly with a hint of tiring of his indecision. "I think you should do what you want to do."

"Okay, say you're my fiancée." He didn't take a breath before continuing. "If you had seen both houses, which one would—"

Sommer stopped him with a waving hand. "I have already said that I like the big house and would buy it if I could. And besides, your beloved wouldn't be seeing these houses if it were a surprise."

"You're right."

"Why are you doing this to me?"

"Doing what?"

"Michael." Sommer was disappointed about his engagement and was confused with his questions. She squinted her big brown eyes as if trying to analyze his motives. And then simply asked, "Can we go now?"

"Yes, but one more question—please. Can we go back to Serendip?"

Sommer looked at him in disbelief. She glanced at her wristwatch. They had been together going on four hours. But the commission carrot was dangling. Even though he was engaged, she enjoyed his company.

"I need to call Alice."

Chapter Three

The day had been sunny and pleasant. A warm breeze was blowing Sommer's hair as she and Michael sat on the stone wall drinking of the beauty before them. Sommer sat with her legs over the wall, and this time, they were five feet apart instead of the ten feet when they were here before lunch. Sommer didn't think what she was going to do as she followed Michael down the front yard. He sat down and she sat beside him. She was still stunned and disappointed about his engagement but was more concerned about the business at hand. It seemed a long time before Michael spoke.

"You know Sommer, if I was to buy this house, here would be my favorite place. I would get some comfortable chairs and my beloved, as you said, would sit here with me and we would enjoy what 'God hath wrought'."

Sommer didn't comment. She knew it was time to press for a commitment from Michael but was enjoying just sitting next to this wonderful man. But what John Oxford, her boss, told her this morning suddenly jumped to the front of her mind and stirred her to speak.

"Do . . . do you need to see the inside again?"

Michael didn't answer. He was at that moment thinking about the big stone fireplace.

"Wasn't Daniel Boone born in Tennessee?"

"What? Daniel Boone? What does he have to do with this house?" She looked at Michael and spoke with the authority of a school teacher. "No, he wasn't born in Tennessee. He was born in Pennsylvania and when a teenager his family moved to the Yadkin River area in North Carolina. I guess he travelled some to Tennessee."

"He had a big fireplace in his log cabin, didn't he?"

"I don't know."

"Yeah you do—remember on TV? His wife, Rebecca, cooked at the fireplace. They had cranes with hanging pots. Just like the fireplace cranes in this house."

"Oh yes."

"Would you like to cook the way Dan'el's wife did? By the way, can you cook?"

Sommer didn't answer quickly, and Michael charged on with, "I take your silence as no."

"No! I mean yes, I can cook. I'm a good cook." Sommer was getting disoriented. She wasn't making any progress selling the house. He didn't seem in any hurry to leave the wall and now he was talking about cooking. As she looked at her watch, he asked, "Does the washer and dryer stay?"

"Yes."

"Didn't you say you had a list of monthly expenses?

"Yes."

"Is it heated with gas or electric?"

"Electric—two heat pumps. I don't remember the size. I have it in my folder."

"That's okay. Now can we go inside?"

"Finally!" Sommer thought.

They spent around thirty minutes looking again at the inside features of the house. There were four bedrooms, each with a bath. Three were upstairs. Impressive, curved stairs connected the main level to a balcony overlooking the great room with a vaulted ceiling. The massive stone fireplace was two stories tall and located on the end of the room facing the front view. To the left of the fireplace was a wall of windows spanning from the floor to the apex of the vaulted ceiling. To the right of the fireplace was a compact kitchen that was part of the great room. Michael and Sommer were standing in the center of the great room, facing the kitchen, when he turned to his right and remarked how convenient the sun room would be for dining during cool weather.

Sommer was getting restless and anxious for a disclosure of his intentions. She couldn't discern if he really liked the house or if he was just a rich guy spending a day amusing himself and wasting her time. But then—he didn't seem like one who would waste anyone's time. And on this side of her thoughts, maybe he was just cautious and didn't want to make a mistake when spending such a great sum of money.

Michael was standing by the fireplace when he softly asked, "Sommer, do think you could cook a meal here."

She walked to the fireplace and moved a crane. "Bet it's hot standing here in the summer." After a moment, "Sure I could. This would be just another source of heat from what I'm used to. Guess I might need some different recipes."

Then she realized he had pulled her from the present to fantasy dreaming that would never happen in her simple life. She wanted to leave. Her boss had told her earlier, in so many words, that if she didn't sell a house soon then she would no longer have a job. Well, right now, she didn't care. She wanted to cry but would wait 'til later—at home. It was almost four o'clock, and she wanted to leave and start thinking about another job.

Michael abruptly shattered her downhearted thoughts. He maneuvered to face her and looked directly into her melancholy eyes as he kindly spoke.

"Sommer . . . would you . . . would you do one more thing for me?" She looked away as he waited for an answer. All day long, she had done everything he asked. She didn't want coffee after leaving the office. She didn't want to have lunch with him. She had sat on the wall two times. He was steering her to . . . she didn't know where. In her mind at this instance, the house sale was not going to happen. But what was in her heart was a different matter. She was actually angry with herself for suddenly being in a love that could go nowhere. She could never be a part of this man's rich family and friends. She would say yes to be with him a little longer and then she wanted him to leave Tennessee and let her return to her unhappy life. Never had she been so ambivalent—so wishy-washy. She looked back to him and nodded. His face lit up in a triumphal smile. She had yielded again and was now really concerned where that nod would take her. Sommer was twenty-four and should be married. She hadn't dated for a long time. Now today, a charming Prince riding in a white Lexus charged into her life. His manner and smile was irresistible. She thought at times he liked her, but then he liked someone else much better. She was lost in the midst of a fairytale dream when he spoke and jarred her back to the present—realizing they were now just two feet apart.

"Would . . . "

Sommer's body jerked as she stepped backward and said, "What!"

Michael tried again just above a whisper. "Would you have dinner with me?"

Before she could respond, he added, "I need to make up my mind. We could discuss—"

Sommer interrupted. "We could talk now."

Michael walked to the big window and then turned to face her. "I'm sorry. I should have asked if you would help me."

Sommer thought, "So what's another hour with him." She was weary but could go another mile. "Where do you want to go?"

"I was thinking Cowboys On The Water—that is if like seafood?"

After a brief hesitation, she answered without any enthusiasm. "Yes that will be fine."

Michael made up for her lack of excitement when he said, "Okay, great—say I pick you up at six or six-thirty?"

"Michael, wait! I'll meet you at the restaurant at six-thirty. Do you know if it's casual dress?"

A deflated Michael said, "Yes."

He guessed he wanted this to be a date and pick her up and maybe meet her mother. But he quickly knew to be grateful for some more time with this beautiful person and to not press his luck.

"Thank you Sommer. I know you are spending a lot of time but a million-four is a lot of money for a house. There must be thousands of houses for sale in this area that would be adequate to raise a family."

She cringed when hearing family. He was going to get married and have children—maybe in this house.

At ten 'til four, they arrived at the office. They didn't speak more than two dozen words during the drive. Michael had decided, before leaving Ohio, that if he met a southern girl he would let his mind and heart have free rein to really test his gut feeling about Kathleen. He did care for her but was being attracted to Sommer in a manner that went far beyond her outer beauty.

Chapter Four

There was no happy smile on Sommer's face when she entered the office. After sitting down at her desk, she told Alice, "I can't figure this guy. I just don't know . . . I'm not sure what he's after. But then maybe I do."

Alice looked at her dear friend with compassion. She had decided not to tell her what Michael said about why he asked her to show him some houses. But now, she would tell her.

"Do you know why he selected you to show him houses?"

Sommer didn't answer. She blankly looked at Alice. What difference would it make if she knew? He was not going to buy a house and she would most likely be working again at the Cowboys on The Water restaurant that she had vowed not to enter again.

"Don't you want to know?"

Sommer pertly answered, "Yes! Tell me."

Alice hesitated before saying, "He noticed in the listings that you had the lowest priced houses and he wanted you to—"

Sommer looked astonished." He said he wanted me to get a big commission?"

"Yes."

"Well, I wish he would tell me . . . I wish he would go ahead and sign a contract. Do you know he wants us to have dinner tonight?"

Sommer stopped, looked out the window, and in a worried tone, asked, "I wonder what he is up to."

She seemed to analyze her last statement and readjust her frame of mind as she walked over close to Alice and whispered, "He's engaged and says he wants to buy a house for his fiancée. He keeps asking my advice and if I like the Zilgler place." Sommer didn't feel like mentioning the Serendip thing. She increased her volume a little, "Now tonight, we're having dinner to talk more about . . . oh, I don't know. But I do know I can't keep him off my mind. I feel so helpless—he's using me, but I'll dine with him because I can't help myself."

Alice was shocked and sorry for her best friend. She had encouraged Sommer to date but to no avail. Now this guy suddenly appears in town sweeping her into a whirlwind of confusion that had her head and heart spinning. How unlucky for her to fall for a man with a fiancée! Alice had, at times, been like a mother to Sommer. Right now, she couldn't think of any wise advice that would comfort her friend.

Rapidly, Sommer started looking in her folder. "Ah yes! Here it is. I'm going to call his office and find out if he can afford a million-dollar house. Alice didn't approve but didn't say anything.

"Hello, my name is Sommer Rose with the Oxford Realty in east Tennessee. Michael Bentley is . . . "

Sommer moved the telephone from her ear when a female screamed, "So that's where he is?"

After a period of giggling, she continued. "Oh boy, what kind of surprise is he up to now? Did you say you're with a realty company?"

Sommer almost hung up but answered, "Yes, he's . . . oh, who am I speaking with?"

"I'm Nita. Is he buying a house?"

"He's looking at a very expensive one—"

Sommer was interrupted again.

In a more normal voice, "Honey, if you're wondering if Michael can afford this house—don't worry. He can afford anything he looks at. Wow! You have made my day."

Sommer listened to more giggling before Nita blurted, "Oh! I have another call. Good luck honey."

Sommer gently cradled the telephone and kept her head down until Alice said, "Sooo . . . "

"So what?"

"I'm asking *you* Sommer Rose."

Moving her head toward Alice but not looking at her, "I just talked to his fiancée. I need to go home."

Without saying goodbye, Sommer left.

Sommer went to the back porch as soon as she could after arriving home. The porch was small but was her cloister—her refuge. She sat with a cup of hot, herbal tea for a long time before her eyes would focus. The yard was landscaped with a few shrubs and a small plot of wildflowers. The view was not necessarily pleasant but was familiar. It often helped her to sooth frayed nerves and refresh a depressed spirit. After twenty or so minutes, her mood had not changed. She went to the porch mad and was still mad. She was mad at herself for calling his office. She was angry with Nita for having Michael.

But one thing she decided—she was not going to dine with that disgusting man—the one who was always so happy and upbeat. But why shouldn't he be cheerful—he was rich and had that tittering Nita to marry.

She picked up the phone. A decision had been made—she was not going to be miserable listening to him talk about the house he's buying for Nita.

"Michael Bentley please." She had already told herself that she no longer cared about the possible sale. She was going to make some new plans—no more real estate. "Michael."

"Oh, hi Sommer, I had just flopped on the bed thinking about you and the surprise house."

He waited for a comment. Sommer was momentarily speechless after hearing his voice.

"Michael."

"Yes."

"I did a bad thing. I feel so ashamed."

"Now wait a minute Sommer. I doubt you could do anything bad."

"Michael, I called your office to—"

"You what? You called my office to check if I could afford the Zigler house?"

"How . . . how did you know?"

"Well now Sommer, I'm in business and investigate potential clients before spending a lot of time with them. Smart people do background checks. So see, you are a smart real estate person."

She also meant to say that she had ruined the secret to surprise his fiancée with a house. But being a smart real estate person was ringing in her ears and she couldn't rationally think how to continue. Suddenly, she realized he apparently didn't know whom she talked with and maybe he would buy the house before he knew Nita knew. She called to confess about checking his credentials and about the secret and to cancel dinner. In less than a minute, she turned her temperament and intentions around so completely that she was embarrassed for calling.

"Sommer, you okay?"

"Yes. What . . . what time are we to meet?"

"Six thirty. Is that okay?"

"Yes, that's fine."

The last few words were mellow and calm.

After ordering, Michael looked at Sommer's brown eyes. They seemed different tonight—darker but clearer at the same time. Her arched brows appropriately crowned the splendor of her engaging brown eyes. Her face seemed relaxed and placid. Earlier today he had seen some stress and strain. But now, four feet from her he was seeing a more pleasing Sommer.

"What is it—why are you looking at me?"

"Oh. Was I looking at you?

"Yes."

"Were you looking at me?"

"Well yes but just—"

Michael put up his hand. "Hey, I was just comparing you with other girls I've known." He waited for a comment. When silence was her remark, he continued looking and asked who she spoke with at the office.

"Nita."

Michael didn't say anything. Sommer didn't say anything. She lowered her head and thought about leaving. She was becoming uncomfortable and guilty about revealing his secret. Some strain marks were beginning to appear. She was back to feeling angry again but only seethed for a second before saying, "Michael, I talked to your fiancée. I said you were looking at an expensive house. I didn't mean to . . . "

"Oh."

"Michael, did you hear me? The house—your secret—I'm sorry. I shouldn't be here. I'm leaving."

"No! No don't leave. This is not bad."

"I don't understand. I blew your plan and I'm truly sorry." He smiled.

"Michael, I have made a problem for you."

"No problem—Nita is not my fiancée."

"What!"

"No, we've had some dates but I have no intentions to marry giggling Nita."

Sommer didn't know if she would laugh or cry. She was glad his secret was intact and sad there was still a fiancée somewhere who would . . . she couldn't finish her thought.

"You okay? Should we leave?"

"No. I'm alright."

She wasn't alright. Her custodial senses were shutting down and she was feeling numb. Again, in his presence, she had the tractable feeling of being a lump of putty. She was ductile. She was being drawn from a resistive demeanor into a yielding mood of 'I'll do anything you ask Michael'.

The food was served, and the format changed from talking to eating. But only a few bites had been enjoyed until Michael broke the silence with a softly spoken question.

"Sommer, do you have a hobby? I mean what do you like to do?"

Without looking up she said, "I have played soft ball for years." She raised her head and solemnly added that she also like to pitch horse shoes.

This wasn't the activity Michael expected from the angel he purported her to be. He leaned a little forward and nodded, as if to imply he understood soft ball and pitching horse shoes were her hobbies.

"So, you have two—"

"No, they are not my real hobby—I like sports, but what I truly like is poetry."

"Wow! No kiddin'? I do too. Oh boy! This is great."

"What do you mean,—this is great?"

"We can recite poems together."

Sommer cast a look at him as if to say, "Maybe I don't want to recite poems with you. And, how can you be sure we will be together? Mister Good Looking Man, you'll soon be married."

Michael read her expression while pressing his lips together. He lowered and tilted his head as wide eyes rolled up like a puppy that had just been scolded.

With a scant smile that acknowledged his regret for assuming, he asked, "Just one?"

She paused and then spoke in a soft cadence.

Abou Ben Adhem (may his tribe increase!)

Michael smiled with a twinkle in his eyes, and with the same rhythm, recited the second line.

Awoke one night from a deep dream of peace,

Sommer said the third line, Michael the fourth, and they continued with alternate lines revealing James Henry Leigh Hunt's reason for writing the poem. The seventeenth line was Sommer's.

And showed the names whom
love of God had blessed,

The good looking guy across the table said the last line.

And, lo! Ben Adhem's name led all the rest!

For a mellow moment, a young boy and a young girl looked at each other as if trying to decide if knowing the same poem bonded them in any special way. The boy was thinking this is a sign that we should . . . He aborted his thought when he remembered Kathleen.

The girl was recalling the timbre of his voice. He expressed the poet's words with spirit and strength. It somehow made her feel safe.

A few more bites and Michael, with his now familiar twinkle said, "How about this one?

If you can keep your head . . .

Sommer finished the first line, "*when all about you*—Hey, every high school kid knows that one. I think its Rudyard Kipling's best."

"I agree."

Michael's food suddenly became tasteless. Kathleen had absolutely no interest in poetry. She had pointedly told him she didn't want to waste her time on some short lines she couldn't understand. Across the table was a person who loved and understood those beautiful short lines. But she . . . Again, he stopped his thought. It seemed that was getting to be a habit.

For the next ten minutes, many poems were recited, including a range from faith and inspiration to reflection and contemplation to home and family and to a soul-stirring one of patriotism. Regardless who introduced a poem, the other one knew it completely or at least some lines. The half-eaten plates of food were totally abandoned as calmness surrounded a couple lost in a mellow slice of reverie they had never before experienced. This interlude from eating was an excursion into a domain of defined mutual interest. In those few minutes, calmness changed to blissfulness.

Sommer was perfectly happy as a consoling, quiet serenity coursed through her veins. A few hours later, she would recall that never before had such a state of tranquility surrounded her and filled her so completely with such a heavenly state of peacefulness. Her mind was stimulated with lofty thoughts as they marched with the meter of each poem. New feelings were kindled as her whole being was gladdened because they had recited lines that had sprung from the warmth of inspired hearts.

They felt the snowy wind blow across the deck of the Hesperus and saw a maiden fair lashed close to a drifting mast. They wandered down memory lane, and then saw the spires of Oxford and their eyes moistened as the Oxford men gave their merry youth away for country and for God.

The varied moods of great poems written many years ago were presently swirling within a rhythmic cloud in their minds and hearts. The quiescence moments just experienced prompted a shy, young girl to wonder if this really happened, or was it just a lovely dream? Before she could decide where she was among the sands of time, Michael's soft words jolted her to the present.

"Here's one. It's named 'Waiting.'"

> *Rosy shafts of light*
> *Mingle with fading blue*
> *Triggering ethereal winds*
> *That will sprinkle evening dew.*"

He could see in Sommer's eyes that she was in a searching mode. He continued before she could say anything.

> *"He waited on a bridge*
> *O'er a whispering brook*
> *Balanced on the parapet*
> *To claim the longest look."*

Sommer slowly moved her head in a negative way. With an expression of seriousness, Michael continued.

> *"Soon, beams from beaten silver*
> *Will softly paint the lea*
> *And he'll run the breadth*
> *When a movement he can see.*
>
> *Stacking moments weigh on his mind*
> *Pressing patience 'til at last*
> *Silent searching thoughts*
> *Garner times of recent past.*
>
> *His heart had been tethered*
> *To a vague and foolish way*
> *Until her sweet and happy smile*
> *Came with hope one blissful day.*
>
> *He repeatedly recited his vow*
> *To stoop and build his life anew*
> *And she's the mortar*
> *To bind the pieces fast and true."*

Michael stopped and leaned back in his chair. Sommer had listened intently and looked at him in a way that beckoned him to finish what she thought was beautiful. She told him her thoughts and asked if he would continue.

"There has to be more. Did she show? Did his hope run to him or did they meet in the middle of the meadow?"

Slowly and seriously, Michael recited the last stanza.

> *"Green velvet slowly glistened*
> *Far as two misty eyes could see.*
> *A beautiful dream was ending.*
> *There was no movement on the lea."*

"Oh Michael! That's not fair. How could you end it that way?"

"My dear Sommer, There are such stanzas in real life."

With a sternness in her expression he had not seen before, she started to speak, but he interrupted.

"Now don't fret. I've written some happy lines."

After Sommer responded with a belated smile, her poet friend, with sternness in *his* expression, asked a question.

"With reference to the poem, have you ever been in love and been rejected?"

She jerked her head up and blankly stared while thinking, "What . . . what kind of question?" They had only met a few hours ago and now this. Sure, they had recited some poems about love, but she was certainly not going to reveal any part of her personal life to someone she just met this morning.

Not giving her time to answer, "I have. I was seventeen." Without her consent, Michael began his love story. He apparently didn't see or chose *not* to see her perplexed expression.

"My Aunt Flo lives in Sandusky, Ohio which is located by Lake Erie. It's a little over two hours from Columbus. Her neighbor, Rachel Buckenberger, asked her if my cousin and I would be a blind date for her niece and friend. My first cousin Robert and I had visited our Aunt often and we knew her neighbor Rachel. We jumped in my red Z28 Camaro convertible and arrived at Aunt Flo's, nine-thirty on a Saturday. The four of us were going to Cedar Point. Do you know about Cedar Point Amusement Park?"

"No."

"Well, well. My dear Sommer, you don't know what you have missed."

Sommer didn't change her apathetic expression. She had not tasted the cheesecake before her. She had been intently listening, and her mind was floating somewhere between the sound of his voice and the impossible dream of belonging to him. Oh yes, she knew what she was missing was more than an amusement park ride.

"Well, let me quickly tell you about . . . " Michael stopped and asked, "I'm sorry. You may not want to hear about—"

But Sommer resigned again to his forceful personality and replied, "Oh yes, go on." She let her dream float away and decided to be practical and take advantage of his presence while she could. "I've never been to an amusement park except at a county fair carnival."

"I bet you would love Cedar Point. Okay, let me see. It was 1995 . . . August. At that time, twelve roller coasters were operating. The Magnum XL-200 was the best known with a top speed of 72mph. The first roller coaster built in 1892 had a 10mph speed—whee!"

Sommer's eyes searched for a reason for being in this restaurant hearing about roller coasters at a place that she swore never again to visit until she remembered the commission. She was hearing, but not really listing to, Michael's enthusiastic comments about the different roller coasters. She later recalled that the Gemini was the tallest in the world and he would later tell her that in 2000 the Millenium Force started operating and was both the tallest and fastest in the world. After his roller coaster dissertation, Michael was silent for several heartbeats.

"My cousin, Robert and I walked into Rachel's living room. Jodi and Beth were standing in the back of the room near the dining room French doors. Without hesitation, Jodi and I walked toward each other, meeting in the middle of the room. We smiled and extended our hands as if we were old friends. In a moment of bewilderment I wondered why I was so lucky for Jodi to pick me. She was really beautiful with long blonde hair and brown eyes. She was many times more attractive than her friend Beth."

Michael stared at Sommer until she averted her eyes.

"Yes, Jodi was beautiful but you, Sommer, are more beautiful in an entirely different way. You have a wholesome beauty that has depth with an intensity of tenderness and understanding and . . . and your eyes shine with honesty and sincerity. And your full lips are so . . . so appealing and inviting and—"

Sommer interrupted, "Michael, you were going to tell me about—"

"Oh yes . . . Jodi."

Behind a sheepish grin, Michael collected his thoughts to continue his story about his first love affair.

"Well I can say we had a special day together. We were both relaxed and laughed a lot and were . . . well, just happy. After an hour together, we had ridden the fastest coaster two times and the thrill of the speed and twisting seemed to attract us to each other in a manner beyond the shyness of a classical blind date. I soon found out that she loved to dance as much as I do. Throughout the day, we danced to park songs to the seeming delight of the onlookers."

Michael lowered his head, and then as if talking to the table, "That's when I knew I loved her. It was the third dancing time."

He looked up at Sommer who looked back with a pensive expression on her wholesomely beautiful face. Her deep, brown eyes seemed to be searching for the reason he was telling her about Jodi. Sommer also loved to dance and wondered how she would feel in his arms. Michael continued gazing at Sommer but he seemed lost in the memory of falling in love with Jodi. Sommer slowly lowered her head pondering if Jodi was his fiancée and if so, why had he waited until now to get married? Her thoughts rambled on and guessed his age to be roughly twenty-four based on the years between his blind date and now. Before she could double-check her arithmetic, Michael spoke with the same timbre as when he knew he loved Jodi.

"Yes, it was a special day. We roamed the park—or I should say we floated through the park doing whatever pleased us. We ate."

Michael paused.

"We played games."

He paused again while looking over Sommer's head. He smiled and then made contact with her beautiful brown eyes.

"We went swimming mid-afternoon."

Sommer was expecting another pause, but he quickly continued, "That's when I kissed her—underwater. I should say *we* kissed—it was mutual."

Michael lowered his head again before continuing with a slight frown on his handsome suntanned face.

"Sommer, I doubt I can convey the glorious feeling—the happiness—the euphoria that filled my heart and mind. I really did feel like I was floating. Some kind of magic encompassed us. There were times when we looked at each other that a hush seemed to surround us to prevent enchanting moments from escaping." Michael briefly closed his eyes as if reliving those intervals of stalled ticks of time.

"As I later thought about our time together it seemed like a beautiful flower from dreamland that fluttered into existence as we enjoyed happy hours."

Michael was again silent, apparently reliving his day with Jodi while Sommer was thinking, "Hey man, stop talking about that girl and talk about buying the house." Sommer was jealous because she was now convinced that Jodi was his fiancée. Sommer looked at her untouched cheesecake. She was ready to leave and placed her hands on the table to stand.

Michael jumped off his cloud and almost shouted. "Oh no Sommer! Please don't . . . "

Sommer lowered her head and picked up her fork. When she looked up, Michael seriously looked at her expressionless face before continuing with some dreamy words.

"It was around 6:00 p.m. when we knew . . . we knew. My teenage hormones were aroused when I first saw her and each subsequent glance and each time we touched continually stimulated them until I was hopelessly controlled by desire. Good sense and my sterling moral values were in the backseat. Seeing Jodi in a bathing suit and kissing her sent them to the boiling point."

The young man who barged into Sommer Rose's life earlier today was about to conclude a story that he had never told another person—a story that would have a consequential impact on both their lives. He would continue without embarrassment because an inner impetus was driving him to share joys of a day in his life that had been in a locked down part of his memory. The unexpected joys that came would alter a part of his life forever. The young, suntanned man looked fully at his dinner companion and candidly stated. "We checked in a nice hotel room."

Sommer stiffened.

"We were both nervous but somehow didn't feel guilty. I guess we were comfortable enough to let torrid hormones decide our action, because an impulse deeper than our previous constraints seized us. The beautiful hours together had wrapped around us so completely that we were insulated from the axiom of right and wrong. It was the first time for both of us.

Sommer pressed her lips together until they disappeared.

"I can tell you it was like I never dreamed could be possible. It seemed I was sailing in a dazzling emptiness, lit only with a shimmer of moonlight. Velvet winds caressed my whole being as I soared and tumbled until Jodi's arms corralled my flying senses."

While Michael was recounting the most blissful feeling he had ever known, Sommer was unaware that she had been slowly leaning forward toward him. When she realized what was happening, she jerked and moved back in her chair. There was silence at table number six in the Cowboys On The Water restaurant. The minds of two young people were searching for some reference to the credence that they were meant to be together tonight. Michael wasn't ashamed that he told Sommer about his day at the park. He wasn't sure why, but he wasn't ashamed.

Sommer sat motionless while blankly looking at Michael. A touch of wistfulness surged through her stunned mind as her thoughts flipped through a chapter in her younger life. Before she could discern the significance of Michael and Jodi's love-making in relationship to his engagement, he softy continued.

"Sommer, I know we sinned, and I have asked God to forgive me, and I know he has. Remember the story in the Bible about King David and Bathsheba?"

Michael waited for a nod from Sommer.

"The Lord forgave David even after he had Bathsheba's husband, Uriah the Hittite, killed in battle. I don't know why I did that thing, except it must have been a boy-girl thing that happens at an amusement park. But like I said, it was the first time for both of us and guess what?"

He paused and then shamelessly stated, "I have a son. He was born May the seventeenth, 1996. His name is Adam, and he lives with Jodi."

Sommer put up her hand as a halt. "I'm confused."

Before she could go on in her state of puzzlement, Michael put up his hand.

"Adam is six, and has always lived with his mother. I have only seen him when he was two and five. I told Jodi I would marry her but she said no. There was no rendezvous on a moon-lit meadow, or anywhere. I waited, but I didn't press her because she seemed so sure of her answer. Jodi was my first love and my first rejection.

Four months before Adam was born, I set up a trust to provide for him through college. My grandfather left me a sizable amount of money and . . . and . . . well . . . That's it. You now know all about me except who I'm going to marry."

During Michael's chronicle of his younger life, Sommer's pallid face showed her astonishment for hearing about a most private event in his life. She felt faint. Her thoughts were jumbled, and her mouth was partially open. She stared at the ketchup bottle a long time before looking at Michael. His eyes were closed, and the contented look on his face seemed to reflect that he was emotionally satisfied and mentally at ease. He began to smile before opening his eyes.

When he saw Sommer's puzzled look, his smile faded like an echo, and he said meaningfully, "Sommer, please believe me. I have never told anyone about what happened that day at Cedar Point. When the Lord forgave me for my sin with Jodi, I also remembered the Bible story about the woman caught in the act of adultery. It's in the eighth chapter of John. When Jesus said, *'He that is without sin among you, let him first cast a stone at her.'* Her accusers were convicted by their own conscience, and they all departed. Jesus had been stooped down writing on the ground, and when He looked up a second time and saw only the woman standing before Him, He asked her *'hath no man condemned thee?'.* She replied, 'No man Lord.' Jesus then said, *'Neither do I condemn thee: go, and sin no more'.*"

Michael's dinner guest didn't respond and didn't change her baffled expression as he continued.

"Sommer . . . I . . . I have followed Jesus' instruction with regard to sex. I have not been intimate with a woman since that first time with Jodi. I don't know why I've told you all this but I'm not sorry . . . I mean . . . "

Before he could finish, Sommer moved to get up. Michael jumped up to move her chair and meekly said, "Guess it's time to go."

"I'm going to the restroom and will be back."

The tears began before she got to the restroom. For a short while, she couldn't control the crying. Only a few hours ago, she met this beautiful man who revealed to her a most private and personal episode in his life. This disclosed to her that he was honest and unreserved and virtuous and compassionate and just totally beautiful inside. With all the discipline she could muster, senses and emotions were gathered and tucked into their proper places. She washed her aroused, flushed face in cold water to cool the embarrassment from listening to his detailed love affair. She wasn't wearing any makeup to repair so she just stood motionless, stabilizing her empathy for Michael while making a major decision. Her life, particularly the past two years, had been mostly confined to self-imposed boundaries. She had cloistered herself within a sphere of abbreviated amusement and achievement. Her life, while living with her mother, had been without promise and hope. She had only performed the chores and duties necessary to satisfy her mother's few rules. But tonight she was breaking out of her nunnery, becoming uninhibited, daring enough to reveal a secret.

When Sommer was again seated at the table, she had subdued her shock. Residual blush from the cold water treatment noticeably enhanced her natural beauty as she looked at Michael with an engaging sparkle. Without stammering, she spoke with softness. "I went to a Labor Day picnic when I was seventeen."

She waited for a reaction or a comment from Michael. He didn't change his expression or say anything.

"I lived near Mt. Airy, North Carolina. Most of the people in the area worked for a large sawmill. Every year, the mill owner hosted a Labor Day picnic at the Community Park that had a large lake. I met Tony Panovich, the football team captain, at the picnic. It wasn't like a blind date because we were in high school together. We just started talking and walking on designated trails through a forest of pine trees."

Sommer wondered if she would finish her story about Tony—but then she knew she would. Michael's expression seemed to indicate that he wanted to hear all about her Labor Day picnic.

"We played softball, pitched horse shoes, won a three-legged race and had lunch. There were no roller coasters to heighten our hormone level—that came while swimming at a wooden platform located in deep water. I was a good swimmer, as was Tony. Our first kiss was also under water. I'm not sure I floated through the day like you did, but it was like no other day I had ever experienced."

Sommer paused again for any comment. She couldn't look at Michael while telling about a day that changed her life. She mostly looked at the table with only brief glances in his direction.

"Well, we swam, played games, walked and kissed throughout the afternoon while waiting for the fireworks. Around 8 p.m., we were walking on a trail with beach towels over our shoulders when Tony veered off the trail into a stand of large pine trees. I followed."

Sommer lowered her head, pausing to find the courage to continue. "I guess everything you said also applied to me. Women, you know, also have hormones that can boil, and the steam can fog the best of moral principles. I also moved some values to the backseat. In a moment of delight, a reoccurring need appeared to be fulfilled. At seventeen, I was shy and lonely and craved male attention. My father died before I was two. I believed Tony really cared for me. He had been courteous, funny, and loving even though he had not inappropriately touched me. I felt safe in his big football arms and thought for sure he loved all of me—not just my body. My emotions were also heightened by the holiday atmosphere, and I surrendered to impulses racing in my mind and body and knew what was going to happen."

In another moment, a man she had known for only a few hours was going to hear the rest of the story.

"There was no hotel room, so Tony heaped pine needles as thick as a mattress. It was the first time for me."

Michael actually blushed himself as he looked at Sommer's reddening face.

Sommer Rose, a twenty-four year old real estate sales person who was about to be fired, was ready to tell a man of a short acquaintance about the most intimate chapter in her life. But he had, and now it was her turn.

"Like you described, I also sailed into a dazzling emptiness with nothing to grasp and stop my tumbling. Had I opened my eyes, I would have seen a real shimmer of moonlight filtering through tall pine trees."

Sommer closed her eyes for a rather long time before speaking.

"I also have a child. I conceived that first time. My daughter is also six years old. We live with my mother."

Sommer had hesitated between short spurts, seemingly contemplating her next statement. "Her name is Lorrie Anne."

When she looked at Michael, tears were cascading down his cheeks. The profoundness of their confessions revealed an intensity of frankness that surprised both of them. Tonight, a bond was being forged between them that neither honestly understood. Sommer thought about leaving, but knew she should finish her story.

"Tony and I would talk some at school but didn't date. I wanted to, but he didn't. I now know that I was just another notch or name on his virgin list. When I told him I was pregnant, he made me feel so cheap. He said, 'How do you know it's my kid?' Lorrie Anne was born in June and after graduation, he went out west on a football scholarship. I haven't seen him since I left high school. He has never seen Lorrie Anne—and never will if I can prevent it."

Shy, quiet Sommer had talked with a boldness that surprised her. She suddenly became weak and was having trouble breathing. But she didn't escape from her boundaries to just flutter around like a butterfly. She had indeed stepped outside her fence, and the new environment was frightening.

Michael Bentley was sitting at this table tonight seriously assessing the direction of his life. He did love his fiancée and was planning to buy a house for her if he could convince his heart that she was the answer to his prayer. But . . . but, . . . just across the table sat a person like none he had ever known. To begin—her face was made up with soap and water. Kathleen's face was painted. Both were beautiful but as converse as yin and yang. He had a notion that their true personalities would also be opposite. He believed he knew Sommer but wasn't yet sure about Kathleen.

After Sommer finished her "seventeen" story, both sat without talking. They would occasionally make eye contact but only for a second. They didn't seem to know what to do next. Two young people who had just shared intimate secrets were afraid to speak or move. They couldn't say what was in their hearts because they didn't honestly know their own feelings. Before another minute of sitting would have been really awkward, Michael stood and walked behind Sommer's chair. In thoughtful words he announced that he had written a poem after his time with Jodi.

"I named it Daily Notes.

> *When before the Lord I stand*
> *Beneath His mighty judgment hand,*
> *He will read the life I chose to be*
> *From daily notes He kept on me.*"

She turned her head and looked up into his moist eyes. He knew she concurred with the four lines.

They silently departed the restaurant. Standing beside her car as moonlight sprayed a golden sheen on her scrubbed face, Michael softly said, "Sommer . . . I . . . I will be . . . " A moment of doubt flooded his intentions, and he looked away because he couldn't finish his statement.

His mind was churning like never before. He had experienced some highs and lows in his life, but this poignant instance was beyond any previous emotion he could remember. He wanted to buy the house so Sommer could use her commission to buy her own house. He had earlier jokingly asked her what she would do with her share of the money if he bought the Zigler house. She quickly said that she desperately wanted to move out of her mother's house into her own little house.

His brain continued to be in a flux of agitation ready to become a mound of butter until Kathleen suddenly appeared in an apparition. She was entertaining friends at the Zigler house. He quickly looked back to Sommer and confidently finished his aborted statement.

"I'll be in your office tomorrow to sign a contract on the Zigler house."

Sommer didn't answer or change her sober expression. Maybe her senses were still numb from their intimate conversation.

It now seemed so simple. Kathleen would have a big house for entertaining and Sommer would have her own house. He didn't consider his happiness with this plan. Before she had a chance to reply, Michael added a codicil to his decision.

"Uh . . . uh . . . there's one condition. Is that okay?"

The girl who just kicked down a fence around her couldn't think of any situation she couldn't handle. Michael waited for her to nod.

"It's . . . it's a request—not a condition or a bribe. It's . . . "

Michael was suddenly without words and he knew why. The moonlight burnished her big brown eyes to a shiny radiance, distracting him so that he momentarily forgot his request. She innocently looked at him, which didn't help him to remember his thought. When he was able to speak, his first word spewed out in falsetto.

"Som-mer."

He tried again. "Sommer, my request is would you decorate my new house?"

"Oh no, I'm sorry—I'm no decorator. No, I couldn't do that. I'm sorry." By the time she had refused, she realized the old Sommer was answering.

"Of course, I'll pay you for it, but that's okay I can find someone else."

Before she could reconsider, he tried to conceal his disappointment as he said, "Is ten okay to sign the contract? I need to have some money transferred."

Again, Sommer didn't answer. Sensations of the evening finally erupted into a wave of dizziness and nausea that almost made her fall. Saying goodnight wasn't happening easily. Michael took the initiative and opened her car door. With no more than a weak thank you, Sommer drove away leaving Michael standing on the parking lot watching her car until it was out of sight.

Their parting had to happen this way.

Chapter Five

Sommer was sitting on the back porch when the phone rang. It was beside her on the glider and rang only one time. She didn't know how long she had been on the porch, but she did know three cups of herbal tea had been consumed. Her thoughts and feelings had recycled so many times that they were twisted, overlaid, knotted, and frayed until she was sure she would never sleep again.

An angel couldn't have said "hello" with any more tenderness and affection.

"Sommer."

Hearing his voice sent her emotions whirling at mach speed.

"I've been thinking . . . but first, thank you for a wonderful evening."

She wanted to say, "Thank you for the most interesting evening of my life." But she didn't.

"Thank *you* Michael."

Silence.

"I . . . uh . . . was wondering . . . "

Sommer interrupted. "Michael, can I tell you what *I* have been thinking about?" The new Sommer had moved front and center.

"Of course."

"First let me tell you that I'm sitting on the back porch looking at a beautiful, authentic Japanese pond-strolling garden with a traditional Japanese entrance gate. My garden interpreted nature in a way to give visual enlightenment while adding a measure of mystique and spirituality. It is a peaceful place to reflect and contemplate."

Sommer hesitated as if to ponder her next words. "The moonlight is bright enough for me to see each gorgeous feature. I can see small multi-branch trees with short twiggy growth. They are called Red Sparrow's Nest. I can see low, spreading Emerald Lace maples. I can see mounds of cascading Red Dragon. Dozens of peonies are thoughtfully placed—Abalone Pearl and Ave Maria are my favorites."

Sommer's delivery was dreamy with a poetic inflection. She didn't know Michael was utterly astounded as he absorbed every word of her Japanese garden knowledge.

"I can dimly see daylilies and clematis in a rainbow of colors. Throughout the garden, hosta, irises, bamboo, azaleas and areas of tufted moss are located in a complimentary manner. Large rocks harboring white water hyacinths dot the pond's edge."

The poetic landscape architect abruptly stopped describing the beautiful garden. She needed some encouragement from the new Sommer's cunning strategy to finish what was burning in her mind. She didn't pause long enough for any comments or questions.

"Now Michael, the moon bridge over the pond is what I've been mostly looking at and thinking about. I have been watching a young couple standing in the familiar, sheltered confines of dozens of cherry trees at water's edge. They have just walked to the middle of the arched bridge and are now stopped. The other end of the bridge is shrouded in a misty cloud. Nothing recognizable or comfortable can be seen in the blurry mist. Anyone descending to the other side of the bridge would be walking into an uncertain future."

Sommer stopped for several seconds garnering courage to continue her thoughts.

"Oh, there's more movement. The boy walks to the other end of the bridge and disappears into the murkiness and the girl turns and walks back to the known security of the cherry trees and to be with her class of people."

There was another period of silence while narrator and listener were recovering from what one said and what the other heard. It was Sommer who took the initiative and asked, "Michael, you still there?"

No answer . . .

"Michael?"

She thought she heard a sniffle when he said, "I'm here."

"You said you were thinking? . . . "

Michael quickly said he would call her back. Sommer didn't know the man she had dinner with was close to being asphyxiated. Nothing had ever affected him like her Japanese garden recital. He had cried when he lost his grandfather and father but he was now bawling. He put his head down and slowly recovered enough to call her back.

"Sommer, I'm sorry about tonight. Could you please forgive me for invading your solitude and causing you to . . . oh, I wish I could back up a few days."

Michael paused and Sommer questionably exclaimed, "You mean you . . . you . . . do you not want the house?"

"Oh no, I mean yes. Yes I want the house. It's just . . . just I have never met anyone like you. You are so perceptive and astute. I will buy the house and then disappear. You will marry and be surrounded with what is familiar and—"

"Michael, I'm so glad to have met you."

It seemed the phase "to have met you" was the prelude to the 'goodbye' he was dreading, but she hadn't finished her thought.

"You have changed my life."

"Changed—how?"

"Confidence."

"Confidence?"

"Yes. I am going to be forward looking and . . . and . . . Well, let me say that you have stirred feelings within me that . . . that . . . well, I guess I had just stopped dreaming."

"Sommer, I apologize for—"

"No! No! Don't apologize. I thank you for—as you say—'invading my solitude.' I've been dormant long enough. Tim Bolling, the mechanic who repairs my car, has asked me several times to have dinner with him. Now I'm ready to accept his invitation. You have Kathleen and a great house and the rest of your life is planned."

Soon after she had sat on the glider, all her secret love for him changed to respect and admiration. The winds of reality had blown her off the fantasy cloud. She couldn't walk across a moon bridge from her simple world to his fashionable domain. Her prayer had been answered for the house to sell and secure her job. She'd be getting her own house but would be forfeiting any chance to be closer to Michael. That Kathleen would be . . . Again, she couldn't finish. When the house contract was signed tomorrow, she knew a part of her would dry up with the ink. The new Sommer would move on in life, living with her own social group. She gave little or no thought to the void that would be left in her life after this angel man departed.

Michael apparently didn't hear about Kathleen, a great house, and that the rest of his life was planned.

"You . . . you are saying that I have changed you and . . . and you are go . . . going to have dinner with him?"

"Well yes, that's what I'm saying. It's just that . . . Well, I mean I have decided to step outside my self-imposed boundaries. I'm going to get my *own* house and . . . "

Sommer couldn't clearly foresee any details beyond her house, so she stopped talking. Michael's future was suddenly also without clear details. He couldn't think of anything to say after hearing about the mechanic. He guessed the movie was over. In an instinctive move, he pressed the rewind button and a flash of scenes whirled in his brain while an ineffable sensation flooded his being. Even the marrow of his soul was soaked as an inexpressible perception of his relationship with Sommer painfully registered in his confused mind. The short time spent with her had been so intense and meaningful and even spiritual. Three hours ago he believed she had become the real answer to his prayer, and Kathleen had been a mistake. Now, just seconds ago, he learned she was going with the mechanic because . . . Michael couldn't finish his thought.

"Michael? You still there?"

No reply . . .

"Hello."

"Yeah, I'm still here."

His mind had exploded, and parts of his entity had flown outward like spokes of a wheel. During his brief interval of silence, he had lassoed most of his various feelings and emotions and then remembered why he called. Maybe his trip south wasn't a good idea after all. He had a house for a future wife who in most ways was found wanting when compared with Sommer. But he did enjoy Kathleen's friends. Several had invested with his company. A twinkling in his fuzzy mind caused him to realize that the house needed furniture.

"Sommer . . . I . . . I just remember why I called. Would you please, please reconsider and decorate the house? I know you can do it and—"

Sommer interrupted. "At the restaurant Michael, I was sure I couldn't decorate a doghouse. But a lot of thinking has passed under the moon bridge since then, and the answer is yes. I will. Or I should say—I will attempt to. I have thought a lot about your house and have some ideas."

"Oh Sommer, you have changed my gloom to happiness."

"What gloom are you talking about?"

"Oh Sommer . . . it's . . . uh. . . you have changed my room to happiness—my motel room. I've been here wondering what to do about . . . "

Michael waited for a reply or comment. When none came, he cautiously said, "Sommer, I have an idea how we could . . . or how you could . . . . What I mean is . . . is we could go to some Knoxville furniture stores and you could . . . I mean I could show you . . . Well, you could get a feel for the type of furniture I like."

Sommer smiled while listening to him stammer. It seemed he was carefully asking instead of his customary dictating or suggesting what they were going to do next. Her smile was short lived. More aggressively, he finished his request.

"Sommer, we could be in Knoxville around four tomorrow and after furniture looking, we could have dinner and discuss—"

"Michael! Two thoughts—I think this is tomorrow. When did you first walk in the office? It seems a week ago, but I believe it was Monday. Right?"

"Right! It was Monday." And then he quickly added, "A week ago."

Michael had revived from his gloominess.

She let the week thing pass.

"The other thought is about coordinating and purchasing. I can't walk through a store and— "

"Whoa! I have already made reservations for you at the Hilton for Wednesday, Thursday and Friday."

"What?"

"Now wait a minute. I can cancel."

"Michael, what do you think I am?"

Before she could finish, he said, "You are the nicest and most cooperative—"

"Stop! I thought my life changed direction tonight and a new Sommer would be fully in charge. Now, you have planned the rest of the week for me like . . . like you've planned everything today." And then she added, "And tonight."

Michael didn't have a comment. All she said was true. There was a rather long period of reticence. Both were appraising their position with the other. Just before Michael was about to say they should forget Knoxville and the decorating, Sommer broke the interlude of silence with a herald of good news in one word.

"Okay."

"Okay what?"

Sommer had a frenzy of thoughts in the past few seconds and decided it may be nice to dine in Knoxville. Softly she answered.

"I will dine with you."

"Thanks. Oh, thank you, thank you. We can finalize plans when I sign the contract. Oh! By the way, how long have you had your Japanese garden?"

After a delay, Sommer embarrassingly answered, "Michael . . . I don't have a Japanese garden—just a few shrubs and some wildflowers."

She hesitated and then said in a more positive manner, "But I will have one someday. Having a Japanese garden has been my passion for as long as I can remember."

"I predict that you will have your passion come true, and with that I will say goodnight. Thanks Sommer. I doubt I can sleep but will see you at ten tomorrow—I mean today."

"Goodnight. See you at ten."

After the papers were signed, Michael said, "Ooookay! That's it. Do I see a smile Sommer?"

She indeed was smiling.

"Not bad for showing me houses one day."

Sommer didn't say anything. Surprisingly, she had slept after the phone conversation and was feeling good about the commission. Floating in her pretty head was the reality that in a couple of weeks, she could be in her own house. She gathered the papers and walked to her desk. Michael followed and asked her to meet him at his car as he walked to the front door. He didn't sleep well, and his head was buzzing with thoughts and speculations about what was going to happen next with Sommer. Well, that is—what was going to happen next between them. He knew she would buy furniture and decorate the house. She would be finished with him in a week or two and would then marry the mechanic. He would disappear from East Tennessee to be with Kathleen. Just before reaching his car, he actually said aloud, "And we'll return to her decorated wedding gift."

Michael Bentley was not happy this morning. But he should be really delighted to be able to present such an expensive house to his beautiful fiancée. He had been confused before but not as disconcerted as at this moment. The conversation with Sommer last night was whirling in his weary mind. He had revisited everything they discussed and was still without a clear inclination to what lay around the next bend in his road of life. As if in a trance, he stood by his car staring at the mountains. His back was toward the office, and Sommer startled him when she spoke.

"I'm sorry Michael, John gave me a little sermon and wants me to be in the office for phone duty the rest of the week."

"What? Didn't he hear me say you needed a three day vacation?"

"If he did, he overruled you."

"Let's go back inside. I need to talk to John."

Michael asked John if he was thinking about retiring. Three minutes later, Sommer began her vacation. John had replied that he would indeed retire if he could find a buyer for the business. Alice was promoted to General Manager and John agreed to work part time. Sommer was speechless as she stared with her mouth open. After some lip movement, she tilted her head while leaning toward Michael.

"You bought the company so I could be off three days?"
"I have to find out if you can decorate."

"Oh Michael, that puts so much pressure—"

"Oh please don't feel that way. I know—I just know you can."

For the first time, Sommer rode in Michael's car to the bank to sign a signature card. He opened a $100,000 checking account in her name. He wanted everything first class and didn't want her to let price hinder her decorating plan.

After the brief time at the bank, an excited Sommer went home to get ready for their Knoxville trip. She restrained her jubilation until out of sight of the office. She didn't care if other drivers saw her thumping the steering wheel and heard her shouting, "I can now have my own house!" She couldn't conceal the good news from her mother and repeatedly honked the car horn before parking. They talked about future plans before her mother showed her happy daughter to the back porch while she fixed sandwiches for lunch.

Sommer sat motionless on the glider with her eyes closed for several minutes. She was trying to capture scattered thoughts and concentrate on her next move but her head was buzzing so that they became more strewn and whirled about in a totally incoherent muddled mess.

She had not thought about what to wear tonight until in her bedroom with only twenty minutes to get ready. The happy Sommer suddenly changed to a sullen Sommer. After moving some floral dresses, she stiffened as her hand touched the hanger of a black dress she had forgotten about. Six months ago, she and Alice went shopping in Knoxville, and in an impromptu moment, budget constraints were blanked from her vision when the black dress filled her eyes. Even if Alice had not raved so about how perfect it was, Sommer knew she had to have that dress. At the time she had no plans to wear it because she never went anywhere requiring anything so gorgeous. But now for the first time, she had been invited to dine in a Knoxville restaurant.

Sommer looked in the mirror and admitted the dress was perfect for her. The straight across bodice was supported by two wide shoulder straps and modestly exposed some cleavage. The front of the elegant garment was beautifully adorned by eight large, pearly white buttons. She lingered a minute as her high school figure was reflected in the mirror. She rotated and was pleased that her sensible diet and exercising had proven worth the sacrificing and tired muscles. She liked what she saw—especially her flat tummy.

Chapter Six

Sommer was on the front porch when Michael arrived right at the agreed time. He slowly got out of the car and stood by the open door. After a moment's hesitation, he spoke.

"Miss, I'm looking for Sommer Rose."

He hesitated again before continuing, "She didn't give me a house number."

Michael looked up the street and then down the street at the four houses in his view and then stared at the most beautiful girl he had ever seen. "She said she would be on the front porch. Do you know her?"

Sommer didn't answer as she thought for an instant, "Do I know this Rose person he's asking about?" The next moment, her mind was reliving the day she knew for sure that she was pregnant. Her mother was noticeably disappointed but was kind and helpful through it all. An old maid aunt cruelly told her she had made her bed—so lie in it. From that day to last night, she had been self-conscious and ashamed of what she had obviously done. She guessed she had been lying in her bed.

She knew two close friends who had sex only one time before they married and didn't get pregnant. Their family and friends didn't know what they had done. But in her case the whole world knew that she had sex. After Lorrie Anne was born in June, some ol' biddies in town even determined when it happened by counting forward three months—making it September. They knew the exact day of conception could be anywhere within a two week period but the Labor Day picnic would satisfy their nosy minds as the likely day of the month. A friend told her this after Lorrie Anne was born. Her objective in life before that enlightening day was not to do sex again until married— that is if anyone would have her with a child. She furthermore didn't make any lofty goals of achievement. Things common and familiar and safe were her forte in life. She had to admit to her heart, however, that some tempting thoughts squeezed in between beats since last night.

She was aware of the way Michael had looked at her and all the compliments and his concern for her. She knew he had planned and schemed to be with her every possible minute since they met. It wasn't just about buying the house. She was conscious that he progressively seemed more attracted to her and had just shown his trust in her with the $100,000 checking account. For the first time in her life, someone believed she was responsible and honest. He had so absolutely convinced her that she could decorate his house that she knew she could and was determined to do a good job to repay him for his faith in her.

Michael looked up and down the street again before stating, "You. . .you know, you are the same height as Sommer. You're thin and . . . and actually more beautiful with your hair pinned up. Would . . . would you like to go to Knoxville with me to browse furniture stores to . . . to . . . "

When she stood in front of the mirror a few minutes ago, she knew her appearance was a cut above how she normally looked in her modest apparel. It also crossed her mind that her attitude had changed permitting her to be more aware of her emergence into the new Sommer.

Since Michael arrived, she had been still and mute like a lovely mannequin. Suddenly, her arms and head became animated as she excitingly said, "I love furniture. Sure, I'll go with you."

Michael coached his unstable legs to walk to the passenger's door. He wanted to hold her hand to assist, but she didn't cooperate and quickly got in the car. She didn't want this time with him to be like a date since he was engaged, and there was no chance for him to love her more than the way a nice man would love a friend. And besides, she had converted her love for him to something less than serious. Her obligation to decorate would be fulfilled. During that time, she would try to enjoy being with him.

Michael was driving the car by rote, for his mind was miles away—namely, Columbus, Ohio. He didn't want to think about Kathleen but he had to. He had to decide if his feelings for Sommer were an infatuation, or was he deeply and hopelessly in love with her. But then he remembered the mechanic. She as much as said she would marry him. His ego was crushed to think she would choose . . . the thought was so emotionally devastating.

A somber ambiance engulfed them in the car. They had been driving for five minutes, and neither had spoken. He had glanced at her two times, and she seemed stiff as she looked straight ahead. As for enjoying this time with Michael, she couldn't rally any reason to smile or start a conversation. As for Michael, "What about Kathleen?" buzzed in his confused head as he glanced again at the angel beside him.

Suddenly, Michael cried out, "See them?"

"Yes. I see a buck and three does—no, four does."

"Wow!"

"Are you a deer hunter?"

"No, are you?"

"Yes."

"No kidding? You could shoot a beautiful deer?"

"Yes Michael—food for the table. We didn't have . . . " She didn't finish as she remembered that Michael was rich and never wanted for anything and wouldn't understand about having to kill pretty deer for food.

He didn't want to spoil the evening by discussing rights of animals to be free from being killed by humans or the embarrassment of having to kill animals for food. The deer sighting had, so to speak, broken the ice.

He quickly decided to change the subject and gently asked. "Have you ever been to England?"

Sommer jerked her head around to face Michael, as if to imply what an unthinkable question to ask. She thought she had told him enough about her that he should know.

She answered with all the bluntness her personality would permit. "No!"

"Have you ever heard about or seen a Bentley automobile?"

She answered with a little nicer no.

"Would you want to hear about the Bentley car and where it is manufactured?"

With warmth coated with concern, she softly said, "Yes."

"Okay. But first let me say it's not named for me." Michael looked at his slightly more relaxed passenger for a comment.

None came. "Okay then, it's made in England. Let's see, where shall I begin?

The extremely expensive and extravagant Bentley (six figures) is made at a factory named Pyms Lane in Crewe, Cheshire, which is located in the northwest region of merry ol' England."

"You been there?"

"Yes, two times, but I've been to England a total of five times. My Dad collected used Bentleys and Rolls-Royce cars. We would roam the country side searching for them. We, of course, had previously located cars through ads and had appointments but found three by chance."

Sommer seemed interested. She had turned in the seat to better look at the narrator. She couldn't imagine a car costing that much.

"You were going to ask how many cars did my Dad have when he passed?"

"Well . . . yes."

"Eleven—six Bentleys, three Rolls-Royce, one BMW and one Jaguar. They are all twenty or more years old but fully restored."

"You said when he passed. Do you—"

Michael interrupted, "Yes, we still have them. They belong to my mother and me."

There was a period of silence before Michael said, "You know, I'm sure you would enjoy a trip to England. The country drives are—"

Sommer finished his sentence, " . . . so beautiful and peaceful. I've seen some TV shows and dreamed about going there someday."

After a moment of silence, "You could you know."

If Sommer detected any hint of an invitation from his statement, her expression didn't reveal it. But deep within her, she may have been honored by the connotation of a trip with Michael to England. This could be because her stiffness was clearly gone as she had turned a little more in the seat and had smiled several times at him. Previous declarations about her intentions with regard to him had been diluting. Maybe she was hasty in saying she would dine with Tim Bolling. She was remembering Michael's reaction to that statement as she noticed the city buildings.

"Well, that didn't take long. Are you ready to start your decorating career?"

"Actually yes—I'm ready to start repaying you for all you have done for me."

"Whoa! You don't owe me—I'm paying you . . . "

"No! I owe you for letting me get my own house."

"But Sommer, you earned the commission."

"Michael, No, I want to . . . "

With his hand waving near her face, Michael calmly said, "We're having our first quarrel."

The mild fury Sommer had generated from their energized discussion burnished her cheeks to a soft, ruby red. After his last remark, it all drained away until her face was pallid. She was embarrassed by the implication it was a lover's quarrel. The car was now parked, and neither spoke for what seemed like minutes.

When Sommer recovered from the "quarrel", she smiled and then said, "Shall we decorate?"

Three furniture stores were visited. She didn't say much during the walkthrough of the first and second. In the third store she came alive with enthusiastic proposals. Michael was impressed with her earth-tone color scheme and especially pleased with her suggested coordination of hues and textures. She chose a large landscape picture with its combination of colors central to the theme of her overall plan. Blotches of burnt sienna highlighted areas throughout the length and breadth of the four-foot by six-foot picture.

The color would be boldly splashed around to accent all furniture and accessories in the great room. Also, all furniture and accessories would be large and substantially stalwart. In Sommer's mind, that was an elementary given. And finally a tiny percent of black would complete the scheme.

The sales associate, Jim Kelly, who greeted them at the third store was a neatly dressed, kindly gentleman. He was a person with a pleasing appearance, and they would soon learn he would help in a confident manner. Michael introduced Sommer as his interior decorator. Jim gazed an extra moment before acknowledging her. Then, he offered his assistance and stayed a respectable distance behind as they admired and talked about the store's exquisite contents.

After one of the discussions with Michael, Sommer beckoned Jim, "What is this color?"

"That, my dear, is blue celeste or sky blue. As you have observed it is not a common, blue shade, even though a blue sky is generally common."

Jim turned to Michael and said, "Sir, I must complement you for choosing this attractive person for your decorator. There has not been a more beautiful woman in this store."

He slowly moved his head to see Sommer blushing, which enhanced her flawless face that was free of cosmetics.

"And Sommer, I have been observing your decorating ability. I have seen some veteran decorators spend hours in here and leave without a competed plan. But you Sommer, have been here less than an hour, and I would say your plan is ninety percent compete."

She looked at Michael who was smiling. He thought about asking, "A penny for your thoughts," but didn't. Before she could comment or collapse, Jim said, "You appear to be happy with your vocation?"

In a moment of bewilderment, she couldn't decide if he meant decorating or real estate. But how would he know about her real estate job?

"But if you are ready for a change," he added, "I suggest you move to Hollywood. You have the beauty and figure to become a celebrated movie star. In the short time I have observed you, I see impressive characteristics that would qualify you for any movie role. And let me add, if I were a talent scout, I would sign you today."

Michael was disgusted with himself for not having said all that to her. He had certainly thought and believed it.

Sommer's emotions reached a zenith; her senses had never been so stimulated. She was motionless and speechless as a blushing heat overflowed from her face to fill her entire body. She couldn't think what to do. She did place her hand on a wing-back chair to keep from falling. Time had either stopped or had warped to another dimension because her mind was so distorted she didn't know if she was standing in the past or future. Some signals from deep within finally made her realize she was in the present. She slowly lowered her head in an abbreviated bow and spoke in a whisper.

"Thank you Mr. Kelly. I don't deserve all you said, but I truly thank you."

Jim Kelly looked directly into Sommer's moistened eyes and said, "It has been a pleasure to have met you Sommer. You and Michael are a lovely couple. He then bowed and turned unvaryingly as a mechanical tin solider and briskly marched away.

Michael and Sommer, soon thereafter, quietly left the store and in continual silence, walked to the car. He was so proud of his decorator that once in the car he believed he was only a touch away from placing Kathleen in the "someone he used to know" category.

Sommer sat in the car and willed with all her might to be stable again. The euphoria of actually being able to put together her decorating plan had filled the center of her thoughts and consciousness to overflowing. Perceptions had become realities before her eyes. And then when a stranger dumped into her mind a breath-taking accolade, she had almost fainted. A passive Michael didn't help. She didn't know he was also calling on all his reserve mental faculties to consummate the decision about Kathleen.

Chapter Seven

They were seated at the restaurant a little before seven. A cool, brisk breeze during the walk from the car helped to stabilize two minds and hearts. Sommer had never pretended to be anything more than a waif from the other side of the tracks. As if by magic, today she became a decorator and was beginning to believe her capabilities far exceeded previous expectations. She now believed she had intrinsic potential and favorable opportunities would come her way. She didn't expect to be a movie star, but every woman should hear, at least once in their life time, what Jim Kelly said today. It may have been flattering to sell furniture, but the part about having her plan essentially complete was true. The bedrooms and baths would be easy because they were also fundamentally finished in her mind.

While in this vaulted state of excitement, Sommer asked Michael to order for her. They talked about decorating until the food was on the table. By that time she had mellowed enough to smile and remark that everything looked good. It was something Polynesian and indeed was good. After a few bites, some energy was restored, and some equilibrium also returned as her senses regained evenness and balance.

Maybe it was a ricochet from the store visit, for suddenly a ghostly feeling was all over her. She was tingling, and her mouth was dry. In an inconceivable vision, she and Michael were on their honeymoon in England. For the second time in a few minutes, she had to beg her mind not to let her explode or faint. Sure, a new Sommer had emerged after last night, but such a bold thought was silly. Before she could decide to leave the table, Michael asked if she wanted to hear more about England?

With a frozen expression of unbelief on her flushed face, she nodded her head and, just above a whisper, answered the handsome man across the table.

"Yes. Yes, I would like to hear more."

Looking at him prompted her to remember about the roller coasters at Cedar Point. In her heart and soul, she knew that since meeting him, she had just been on one bigger and faster than any he described. And at this instant, she was ready to climb aboard another one for an international ride.

Michael gazed at the floor a long second before starting.

"One reason I love England is because it's so ancient and regal. You know some of the history—like the wars and kings and queens. It's all of those olden time events that sort of wrap around me when I'm there. I enjoy some of the cities and towns, but it's the open country for me."

Michael had been looking directly at his lovely dinner guest and was suddenly overwhelmed again with her beauty and couldn't speak. He wondered if she would let her hair down—but he realized she was lovely with that hair style too.

"Is that all?"

"Uh…uh, oh no."

Of course there was much more, but he was having trouble concentrating as flashes of what Jim Kelly said bumped into words of his narrative.

"In the cities, I like the beautiful brickwork of the Victorian factories. I don't like the traffic. But it must have been a lot worse round about the intricate network of canals and railroads during the Industrial Revolution and the Second World War. Okay, after busy inner city streets and leafy suburbs, my favorite place comes in view—the open countryside."

Michael lowered his head and stared at his plate for a few seconds. It seemed his thoughts were being set aside from the hustle and bustle they had experienced today.

"You drive along rolling curvy roads with a spacious panorama of estates and plots bound with fences and hedges built and planted in a bygone era. The vista and fragrances and sounds of the seasons can't be fully enjoyed from a history book or a novel. You have to be there to see the dozen shades of green and smell the new cut hay and hear the groaning of a distant tractor. When talking with the farmers and rural people, I have a strong sense of my English legacy. It's like I belong there working alongside them making hay like I did on my grandfather's farm."

Again the storyteller hesitated. Then, in a tone reminiscent of a former time when living was at a slower pace, he continued. "You know Sommer, sometimes I've been driving with the top down at forty miles per hour, and imagine I'm in a horse drawn coach going four miles per hour. I'm dreamily transposed to the time when genteel people lived in a comfortable, cultured world and entertained relatives and friends for weeks at a time. At my imagined four miles per hour gait, I pretend to be on the way to an uncle's estate where there'll be dancing 'til dawn. And if I'm lucky, you will be there, and we will dance together."

Sommer was listening but not looking directly at her dreamer friend. She was also envisioning the coach ride and the extravagant, continuous party with an abundance of food and graceful dancing. When she heard "dance together," she quickly looked at Michael with a bemused expression.

He smiled until she lowered her eyes. Then, with less wistfulness, he said, "Like in the movie, *Pride and Prejudice*."

"Oh Michael! That's my favorite movie—well, one of my top five."

"How many times have you seen it?"

She tilted her head and answered with a squeak, "Three."

Without embarrassment, Michael replied, "I've seen it four times."

They both turned on a consoling smile. Michael's smile suddenly vanished as he rather loudly remarked, "You know what that makes us?"

"Well no, unless it makes us people who like to watch movies about—"

Michael interrupted. "No! No! Well yes, but it's deeper and more profound. More, more meaningful—it connects us in a special way. You see? We are kindred-spirit friends. We are of the same sort because of our similar interest in the custom and manners of that period. I should have realized this when we were reciting poems. We are of the same sort."

"Oh! Also like in Anne of Green Gables—another of my favorite movies."

"Yes, it is also one of my favorite."

"After the first time seeing it, I wrote a poem."

"I'm not surprised. You have quoted lines and verses of famous poems the past two days. This poem you wrote, is it—"

Sommer interrupted, "No, and never will be, but maybe in a hundred years, someone will quote it while dining in a nice restaurant."

Michael turned on his charming smile and then seriously asked, "What's it about? Will you recite it for me?"

Sommer's expression indicated she was pleased that he wanted to hear her poem. "It's about Anne and Mr. Cuthbert. It's been a while—give me a minute."

"Does it have a title?"

"Yes, I call it No Sweeter Love and in parentheses below—An orphan brightens his life."

The poet briefly closed her eyes and then began with words as soft and tender as the way one would expect an angel should sound.

> *Bands of saffron slip from a nursery rhyme page*
> *As vermillion and gold ride the breeze*
> *All strutting for prominence on a twilight stage*
> *But only his kindness she sees.*
>
> *She was a kindred spirit sent from God*
> *A providential gift for his late years*
> *So his appointment beneath cold sod*
> *Would follow warmth of happy tears.*
>
> *With youthful zeal and dreams she filled her days*
> *Knowing naught his thoughts within*
> *But he knew his fate and cared in driven ways*
> *And no sweeter love has ever been.*

A young man and a young woman sat in a kindred-spirit glow with one wishing their connection could be more romantic than mere special friends. The young man had just purchased an expensive house for someone he didn't love any more. Well there it was. He just admitted to his heart that he didn't love Kathleen. And also in his heart, he knew that after only two days he was genuinely in love with Sommer, and Kathleen would not live in the house. At that moment—at that precise moment of truth, Sommer was the answer to his "find a wife" prayer. Kathleen was a pretty illusion who did not possess the important substance and character to partner through life. Michael silently and reverently thanked the Lord for sending Sommer as a yardstick to measure the deficiencies in Kathleen. He may never be any more than a friend to Sommer, but he knew that Kathleen was history. And the house—it was, for the present, in the blurry mist at the end of the moon bridge.

The young woman's stomach was upset from the day's roller coaster rides. Her heart was so confused that her body seemed to be spiraling downward into a vortex without a bottom. Her senses and logic were twisted into a tangled helix. In her emotional whirlpool, there was such a feeling of anxiety that an unpleasant nervousness was all about her as she anticipated what could happen between her and this handsome young man.

Sommer Renée Rose had never felt this way before. In an instance of unexpected reverie, some scenes from an unexciting childhood paraded by her hazy consciousness. She would lie on the grass and watch cloud shapes change and make believe she could see a Prince Charming charging on a white horse to take her to his palace. She would never get to the part where she would live happily ever after, because she would always cower back to the reality of her station in life and not dwell on impossible dreams.

And now tonight through misty eyes, she saw a Prince Charming five feet away. But by her firm convictions, he was as elusive as the ones in the clouds. She had never before been this close to one of her princes but was still resolutely convinced she was not worthy for palace life.

While these thoughts rambled through the crowded minds of two young people, eye contact was unflinchingly maintained.

It was as though something greater and bigger than they were mesmerized them and then cataloged and arranged their thoughts according to their desires and hopes. Michael had decided and surrendered to the burning revelation in his heart that Sommer was the answer to his prayer. Sommer, in these few ticks of time, had concluded she could not follow her heart and love him forever. It was the underlying fear that she could not measure up to his social level that prompted her decision.

"Oh Sommer—I don't know what to say. Your poem is so beautifully composed and touchingly accurate. You have precisely written a truthful representation of their relationship. Miss Sommer Rose, you may not know it, but you are a poet."

Exchanges of smiles seemed to soothe their rippling thoughts. "Hear that?"

"Yes." Her answer was plainly stated without any enthusiasm or keenness of interest.

The dining room was "L" shaped. From their table, they could see the beginning of the short leg of the "L". Michael moved his head in that direction and swiftly returned to again face Sommer. Instead of a solemn stare, he had a twinkle in his eye.

"That's a five or six piece band."

Sommer didn't concur or disagree.

Michael asked to be excused and went to investigate the music source. He returned and stood beside her chair. With mellowness, he asked her, "Want to dance?"

"Oh no! No, I couldn't dance tonight."

"I thought you loved to dance."

"I do, well I did. I haven't danced since high school."

"Then it's time to do some catch up."

"Oh no! I would step on . . . oh no."

Michael remained by her side and placed his hand on her chair back. She looked up at him again with an expression as if to say, "I want to but am afraid of what might happen." Her soon to be dancing partner was persistent and didn't move. When she placed her hands on the table, he started to move the chair. He wanted to help her stand, but she exited the chair from the other side and stood unaided.

Chapter Eight

It was only a few steps to the dance floor, but to Sommer it seemed as long as a football field. A fleeting picture about another short walk among big pine trees flashed into her memory. A hard lesson was learned from that Labor Day picnic saunter. She had innocently believed Tony loved all of her and not just what he could glean from a virgin. She learned about male ego that day.

She had no problem trusting Michael to remain the caring and compassionate gentleman she had grown to love in two days. She didn't believe he had one egotistical bone in his body and knew he loved her but didn't fully understand why. He could have many other girls far superior in every way. She was not afraid of him, but frightened that she would drop her guard and commit to putting herself in an uncomfortable situation with his high society family and friends. She was terrified thinking about meeting and being with his mother.

The short walk for Michael was a joyous stroll as senses heightened with each ambling step. He had not even touched her hand—but soon, he would hold her hand and then hold all of her in his arms. When they got to the dance floor, thoughts of her imminently being in his arms suddenly made him dizzy.

The band was playing "Stranger on the Shore." A tense couple rigidity stood as statues. Michael let his eyes behold the beauty before him as if searching for a signal to initiate the first maneuver. Sommer's muscles were taut while waiting for her partner to make that first gesture. The assertive, young, suntanned man from Columbus, Ohio, who had executed planned activities for the past two days, could not persuade his arm to rise. Before they would be embarrassed for just standing, the music stopped.

When Michael earlier investigated the music source, he spoke with the band leader and requested a certain song. A cold chill sent paralyzing ripples through him when the music of "The Loveliest Night of the Year" filled the room. Again, he couldn't move. But then the something "greater and bigger" of minutes ago gently nudged him to move closer to the loveliest girl in the world.

When he touched her right hand with his left hand, all the ripples seemed to intensify, but he inherently moved his right hand and placed it on her shoulder. In an equally natural move, her left hand contoured his right arm. For an instant they stood tall, facing each other. After a slight head movement to the left, Michael moved his left foot forward, a slide with his right foot, and then both feet together. Then it was backward with his right foot, slide with his left foot and feet together again. Though it had been years since Sommer last danced, the rhythmic movement of body and feet was a permanent module of her inner being, and she had not forgotten how to follow. Aside from some stiffness and nervousness and not wanting to get too close to her partner, she was again dancing.

Michael moved his left foot for ***one***, a slide with his right foot for two and then feet together for three. Then backward with his right foot for ***one***, slide with his left foot for two and feet together for three. With the precision of a clock, they moved by rote.

He knew the lyrics and silently sang them as his heart swelled with the cadence of the music.

One *two three—**One** two three—**One** two three—*

The music in three-quarter time was slow, sweet, melodic, and fluid with no heavy percussion or drums. The clarinet and tenor sax carried the recurring rhythmic beats. With a smooth progression characterized by long, flowing steps and continuous turns, they were gracefully and elegantly gliding around the floor almost effortlessly. Each rise and fall was like gentle waves of a silk scarf in a twilight breeze.

The sweeps around the floor were sprinkled with lavish open movements, underarm turns, and solo spins. The expressive quality of the five piece band encouraged vibrant and graceful moves. The circles around the floor kept getting closer to the sidelines. The two remaining couples joined the spectators marveling at the beauty and charm exhibited by a handsome young man and his lovely partner.

One *two three—**One** two three—**One** two three—*

On and on, they flowed with continuous sweeps around the floor with open movements, underarm turns, and solo spins. Each time Sommer returned to the handsome young man's arms, their bodies would touch. Not just touch but softly collide. Sommer's initial avoidance of closeness to Michael had dissolved and had been replaced with a desire for them to merge into a single being. Unwavering eye contact, inches apart, sent signals to their hearts that neither had before experienced.

The charisma of the lone couple on the floor did not escape the attention of the band leader. He had been observing dancing for many years but couldn't remember such poise and grace. A pleasant thought prompted him to play the song again as he believed this boy and girl belonged together.

Somewhere, on this Tuesday night of October 2002, some hearts were lonely, some hearts were mourning, and somewhere it was raining. But here on this dance floor, Michael was sure the hands of God were encapsulating them within His loving promise of them being together eternally. No other person could be happier than he as Sommer returned to his arms from a solo turn. A snippet of the lyrics filled his heart that perfectly described his emotional response of love and tenderness toward Sommer.

> *So kiss me my sweet . . .*
> *It's the loveliest night of the year.*

When the music stopped, a man on the sidelines shouted, "Hey man, kiss her!" All in the room, including band members applauded. The celebrities stood frozen in a place and time momentarily out of their scope of understanding. They had danced to a rather slow tempo of thirty beats per minutes but inwardly they seemed to be spinning faster than the speed of sound. It took another "Kiss her" cry before the magnetism of love drew them together.

Since the Celestial Bureau of Standards of Kissing was established, a Recording Angel has been tirelessly scoring every kiss as compared to a perfect "10" kiss. Each observation also considered the degree of compression exerted between the two bodies during the embrace. The Angel wasn't privy to circumstances leading to the kiss but had the ability to measure the eagerness and fervor when lips first touched. This initial impact on recipients accounted for seventy percent of the final score number.

The room was suddenly quiet.

Beyond showing mere kindness and charity to each other, two hearts and minds were united with exhilaration above all expectations for Michael and a conclusion to pent-up frustrations for Sommer. When he first tasted her full lips of natural beauty, nothing in his life before had come close to the happiness that surged throughout his body. Sommer freely yielded to her amorous affection for this beautiful man as they were pressed together near maximum compression. But in a tremor of passion, she locked her right leg around his left leg drawing them even tighter together.

The untangling of arms and legs was in slow motion.

Their moment of ecstasy had lasted no more than twenty seconds. Not long as time of man is counted. The aftershock had already started when they heard the applause. They didn't feel like Rhinestone Cowboys on a Star Spangle dance floor but had the presence of mind to bow before walking away.

Michael dropped a large bill on their table, and they continued in silence to the car.

A dozen—no, a hundred or more times, Sommer wanted to fling herself on Michael and declare she couldn't live without him. She had never been so dazzled. The brilliance of the wonderful evening (she knew) would linger in her heart 'til her last breath. The mute driver had similar thoughts. Only when they stopped at Sommer's house were there audible words within confines of the car.

"Sommer—"

"Please. Please don't say anything about the dance. I want to thank you for a lov . . . a beautiful evening."

Those few words were delivered by a bewildered Sommer who was tense and afraid to admit she was in love.

"Sommer, there's a change in my plan. I don't want the house unless you go with it."

Before he had finished, her glare of disbelief reflected the words "I don't want the house." When "unless you go with it" registered, disbelief was overwhelmed by a desire to fully surrender. But she didn't, and she didn't know there was a Celestial Bureau to record "it might have been" consequences of such a decision. In a blur, all her fears surfaced and all accepted standards of following ones heart to happiness were not seen in the haze. Could it be a "10" was posted for the kiss and now a "0"?

Silence again.

Before she burst into crying, she softly said, "I'll go in and get the checkbook."

"No! No! I want the house decorated and then I'll sell it."

He couldn't presently think clearly about anything. Why should the house be decorated? He could sell it as is.

With a little more firmness in her voice, "I'll leave for Knoxville early tomorrow, and thanks again for . . . I need to thank you for . . ."

Sommer opened the door and a deflated man from Columbus, Ohio knew not to jump out and walk her to the front porch. Before the door was closed, he told her to call him anytime concerning the decorating.

He sat staring over the steering wheel for several long, lonely minutes before slowly driving away from the best and worst day of his life.

Chapter Nine

Sommer didn't sleep well. The clock showed ten minutes until four o'clock before physical fatigue overpowered her churning mind. Michael never tried to sleep. Instead, he drove to Columbus through the night.

At five minutes after ten, she greeted Jim Kelly good morning. The eventful yesterday with Michael was mostly secondary to her mission at hand. Surprisingly, she was energy filled and eager to launch her decorating career. She didn't really consider herself a decorator but had given her word, and the job needed to be finished. After three hours at Jim Kelly's exquisite furniture gallery, the novice decorator left, confident that her plan was attainable.

Many stores remained to be explored. She was looking and taking notes today and would start buying sometime tomorrow. She had done her homework and prepared a schedule of stores to visit. From the beginning, when selecting an item for purchase, she only thought of Michael and what she knew of his preferences. In her mind this was a business thing not associated with romance. Sometime in the wee hours of last night, she had mixed the pulp of her stupid decision with regretful tears and made papier-mâché. This was used to fashion a twisted, broken heart to place on a back shelf in her dim-witted brain. She was thankful for the decorating priority that was preventing the full backlash of last night.

It was six o'clock p.m. before a tired decorator returned to the Hilton. When entering, the aroma of food prompted her crowded mind to remember she had forgotten to eat lunch. The day had been so intense. She later ate while in bed reviewing notes and brochures. Pieces of her master plan were precisely fitting together.

Thursday was a blur—many, many decisions and many checks to write. Friday morning was no different but with much more anxiety. She didn't want to but had to call Michael.

"Hello."

"Hi Michael . . . " There was no hint that her heart skipped a beat when hearing his voice.

"Are you all right?"

"Yes, well nooo . . . "

"What's wrong? Do you need help?"

"Oh Michael, I hated to call . . . "

"What is it! Do you need me?"

"Yes, I need—"

She didn't get to finish because Michael practically shouted, "I'm on my way!"

"No! No Michael—I need your advice."

"Oh." With concern he asked again, "Are you all right?"

"Yes, I'm finished except for one most important item."

When he didn't comment, she continued to tell him about an area rug she found for the great room. She told him about her two hours looking for an alternative. He interrupted two times, but she persisted and finished telling about how she got the price reduced by five thousand dollars, but she only had fifteen thousand left and there were still some little things to buy.

"Please believe me Michael; I tried to find one as nice for less money. Oh Michael, the room can't be compete without this gorgeous rug."

Sommer didn't hear anything.

"Hello Michael. Are you still on the line?"

She had never had such a stressful day with so many major decisions to make. She had made some last minute changes based on the colors in the rug. Just before she felt like exploding, a voice shocked her back to a more stable condition.

"Money is on the way. I'm putting twenty thousand more in your account. Nita is doing it right now."

Now it was Sommer who didn't speak.

"Are you still there? Hello?"

"Yes. Thank you."

She was relieved but more apprehensive because now all the jumble of pieces had to exactly fit together. All arrangements for large item deliveries, early next week, went smoother than expected, but she was suddenly worried that her master plan wouldn't be compatible with the house. She had selected the aggregate items in accord with the beautiful finished plan in her mind. But now she was frightened. She had no mistakes to avoid because with no experience, she didn't know if any had been made. Sommer Renée Rose was guided only by her imagination and a driven desire to please.

Michael asked when he could see the house. He briefly told her about the Columbus weather. She thanked him for the nice accommodations at the Hilton. He asked about Alice.

The conversation was about business and trivial. The fact that Sommer had many times the past three days wanted to totally yield to her heart with "I love you" wasn't mentioned.

Forgiven

A tired and bewildered young lady left Knoxville during Friday rush hour with the trunk and backseat loaded with sundry items for bedrooms, baths and kitchen.

Sommer thought selecting would be the bigger part of her endeavor—wrong. The first truck arrived at noon on Monday. The last delivery was late afternoon Wednesday. She was back in Knoxville Thursday morning. By Sunday evening, aside from shopping locally and out of town, she had spent an average ten hours a day at Serindip. She had barely slept. Hues, shades, textures and shapes whirled behind closed eyes until she felt like screaming.

Michael was coming Tuesday the twenty-second to see his decorated house. That gave her eleven days for delivery and set-up. Deliveries were finished Thursday, and she set up and arranged through Saturday. Another trip to Knoxville on Monday and then final touches 'til after dark. Sommer slept nine hours on the eve of revealing the greatest achievement in her life because a concerned mother practically forced her exhausted daughter to take a sleeping pill.

A celebrated playwright couldn't have been more proud and satisfied before the opening night of a Broadway Play. It had been a stretch. By strokes of brilliance, changes were made and newly inspired perceptions were added to embellish the plan.

Chapter Ten

"Nervous?"

"Yes."

"You like that young man?"

"Yes mother, I do."

"Have you told him?"

"I'm thinking—oh, I don't know. I've got to get through today before I can think straight about anything. Jim Kelly is coming today, and Alice also wants to see the house. I don't know how to arrange it because I want to be alone with Michael when he first sees it."

"Why?"

Sommer didn't answer. She turned and looked out the window.

"The answer isn't in that window—it's in your heart."

"I know Mother. I know but . . . but . . . it's . . . well I guess I want to know if he really likes what I've done. With Jim and Alice there he may not . . . You see what I mean?"

Mother didn't immediately comment. When she did it was a question.

"Could you have Jim go to the office, and then he and Alice could come to the house after you and Michael look it over?"

"Oh mother! Yes, that would work."

Sommer made the phone calls and left her mother's house to begin another new chapter in her life. The short drive to Serendip was over before she could organize her thoughts about how to present the house. But then—what was there to do—just open the door.

According to her plan, she arrived an hour early and made some tea. While the water was heating, she walked to the fireplace and moved a crane. Hanging from each of the four cranes was a cast iron utensil—a dutch oven, a covered skillet, a large pot and a tea kettle. For a reflective moment she thought of Rebecca Boone. She pictured her and Daniel in their period dress and surmised they were happily married. She felt sure the two came from the same frontier area and had no social class differences.

She closed the door and slowly walked to the edge of the front yard and sat on the stone wall viewing the gorge. The breeze was cool but refreshing. The soft murmur of the stream below was pleasant and calming. This was the first time in over a week that she had time to relax. Minutes ticked away as a menagerie of thoughts rambled in her mind. Soon all mental activity centered on Michael. She didn't remember when the tears started, but she did remember that her mother would often say, "No need to cry over spilled milk." She had said no to his proposal, and again she made a bed and would have to lie in it. Her mind was presently in as much stress and galloping turmoil as after the dance. She had a notion to just fall forward off the wall into the gorge—so much for peaceful relaxation.

She was thankful for the decorating because there were times she didn't think about him. As oft before since meeting him, she corralled her emotions and dried her tears—just before hearing his car. She wanted him to sit on the wall with her for a few minutes, and then they would look at the house. She wanted to see his initial reaction because she knew the once vacant house was now beautiful. As he approached, she wasn't so sure being on the wall with him was a good idea.

Without a word, Michael sat close beside her and put his arm around her shoulders. The hug lasted just a few seconds and then he moved a foot away. He knew something—something greater than he could presently understand was still connecting them in some decisive way. He had already ripped the Kathleen pages out of his life and thrown them in a basket labeled mistakes. He was now sitting beside the most beautiful girl in the world. He added a codicil—beautiful inside too. Sommer wasn't tense and she didn't flinch when he lightly pulled her to him. They had embraced and kissed, thereby moving them up a rung on the ladder of love. Both said hello with abbreviated smiles.

"So! How are you?"

"Tired."

"Oh, oh—the decorating?"

"I suppose. There were so many things to do, but I enjoyed every minute."

Both looked into the deep gorge. Both were silent. Both were waiting for the other to speak. A sudden wind gust blew Sommer's shoulder-length hair in her face. As it was happening, Michael turned and, in an impromptu move, parted the blonde strands with his hands. In another unplanned action, Michael softly asked, "May I kiss you to thank you in advance for decorating my house?" Cupped in his hands with only inches between them, she could see begging in his eyes. She had a similar thought about being thankful for the chance to decorate.

When she didn't answer his question, the short distance between them slowly became shorter and shorter.

That Bureau of Standards angel must have seen zillions of different styles of kissing. The kiss just witnessed was no different from millions within the past hour—maybe within the past minute. But for Michael, it was definitely different. Not for any unique style, but dissimilar for what happened to him after their closed lips softly touched. He was no stranger to kissing, but now it seemed a thousand nerve endings in his lips were touching an equal number in her lips. A multi-circuit connection was completed. Uncontainable impulses were simultaneously making a linking association between two pounding hearts. He could feel a succulent fervor radiating from her pure, intrinsic qualities concentrated deep within. Calming warmth flooded his whole being. This soft kiss (with no embrace) was exceedingly more beautiful than the one after the dance, which he had considered the epitome of classic kisses. This tender kiss was savored by Michael for a sweet measure of blissfulness unlike any other time in his life. And he knew why—time had stopped. Nothing had affected him this way before. He was experiencing many firsts with this earth angel.

Michael's consoling smile greeted Sommer when she opened her moistened eyes. She answered with a partial smile because momentarily she wasn't sure if this was a dream or real. Before she could decide, Michael whispered, "I love you." In a reflex from the fire still smoldering in her trembling body, she whispered, "I love you."

Michael's smile burst into a full face of radiance. Sommer's face was expressionless as she closed her eyes again. His sparkle was gone when she opened them. She couldn't stop the tears when seeing the sadness and disappointment on his face.

"Oh, don't cry. I shouldn't have insisted we kiss."

He was about to gather her in his arms when she managed some tear soaked words.

"I'm sorry Michael. I meant what I said but . . . ."

"That's okay. That's okay. I und . . . ."

He almost said understand. But he didn't understand how she could say I love you and then not follow through.

Sommer stood and tried to smile. Michel tried to smile as they turned toward the house.

Michael's initial comments weren't even close to what she expected. Enough was said; however, to convince her he liked the downstairs. When they came down from upstairs, he was calmer and she knew his praise was sincere but nothing like the enthusiastic response she had envisioned. The decorating endeavor had bounded her to delightful heights of satisfaction. But now as Michael looked around the room, all her effort and moments of inspiration seemed secondary to him. He first wanted her, and the decorated house would follow. She wanted the house to be the main subject and after that—she didn't know, except not to get more attached to someone out of her class.

Michael was saddened and Somme was disappointed. They were sitting at the bar when they heard laughing—the only sound in this beautifully decorated house for over a minute.

After a slow sweep of the room, Alice gushed, "Oh Sommer! It's beautiful. It's gorgeous."

Jim Kelly added, "And so stately."

Sommer was walking toward Alice who said, "No, you and Michael stay there. We will walk around and admire. They did walk around the great room and then the master bedroom before going up the stairs. Most of the admiring, however, was toward each other. They had entered the house holding hands and would leave after five minutes still holding hands. Jim Kelly had not changed his somber demeanor during the short time Sommer had known him. She thought his bearing was stiff. His moves were predictable as if each were programmed. Now, with Alice by his side, he was a different tin soldier. He laughed, slumped, wiggled, and pranced about as if re-programmed with new batteries installed.

Some niceties were exchanged when Jim and Alice left for Knoxville. A disoriented couple was then alone in a dream house. Sommer was one word or thought from tears. Michael didn't honestly know what to do next. He did have a plan before arriving but now he guessed it was time go and leave his future behind. Before announcing his departure, he looked around the room and then took a few steps to one of two tan leather club chair and sat with his legs on the matching ottoman. He waved to Sommer.

"Come, sit in your chair."

He saw a look of defiance. Well, he guessed this was the last straw. Now he knew it was time to go. There didn't seem to be anything left to lose so another statement wouldn't matter.

"This really could be your chair."

Sommer didn't move. She was afraid a step would jar tears that might not be easy to stop. Or worse—she might blindly yield to a voice inside her heart instead of her head. Glued to the parquet floor, she watched Michael walk to the fire place and move a crane. He then slowly turned toward his mute friend.

"You know Sommer? I've had just about everything that I have ever wanted. I always received the latest and most expensive toys and had the best and shiniest bicycle in the neighborhood and the first motor scooter. I had a new car when I turned sixteen. I have had a good life and presently have a good job. I have this beautifully decorated house, and most people would think I'm a happy man."

"Please, please don't say anymore," Sommer begged.

"Please don't say I have made you unhappy. I don't ever want to hurt anyone. Oh Michael, I'm the one. I'm the most unhappy person in the world. I wish you could understand my situation. I wish—"

Michael interrupted with more sarcasm than he intended, "I wish I could!"

Sommer closed her eyes as disenchantment drew all color from her face. In a pleading tone without looking at him, she whispered, "Please Michael don't be angry with me."

He rushed to her side and locked his arm in her arm.

"I'm sorry. I'm so sorry. Please forgive me."

He could feel her stiffness.

"I want to understand your thoughts more than anything else in this world."

In an aggressive move, he nudged and she followed to the other club chair and sat on the arm facing his chair. In a spin as graceful as a dance step, he moved the ottoman and sat in his chair beside a sadden angel. The joy that filled his heart when they kissed on the stone wall was gone without a trace and replaced with a hollow feeling overflowing with anxiety. He likened this moment to a tied baseball game—bottom of the ninth with a man on third, and he's at bat with a three-two count. He quietly begged the Lord to help him understand about this angel. He could see the ball coming but wasn't yet ready for what could be a last swing.

In a flash of inspiration, a desperate Yankee boy stopped the ball and asked Sommer a question.

"Have you seen the movie *Mr. Holland's Opus?*"

There was no reply from the full lips that a few minutes ago propelled his body and soul to a dimension of immense delight. Her face was mostly blank but her eyes showed she was wondering what that movie had to do with her unhappy status. She wanted to leave and stood to do so.

"Oh no! Please, please let me finish—*please.*"

The beseeching timbre in his last 'please' caused her to sit back down. Not on the arm but in the chair. Michael moved to stand in front of the fireplace.

"Mr. Holland was a high school music teacher who unself-ishly taught about much more than just musical notes on a sheet of paper or how to play an instrument. He counseled, advised, and inspired with earned wisdom from mistakes of his own younger life. His commitment to his students, including their personal needs, greatly interfered with his personal passion to write music. He was liked and respected by the staff and students. One senior fell in love with him."

Sommer appeared to be listening. Her expression had gradually changed from impassive to more normal until "fell in love" was said. Disapproval was seen in her eyes.

"Please bear with me. I have something important to tell you."

He waited for an acknowledgement to continue. Sommer looked into his begging eyes and said, "Okay" as she nodded.

"This girl wanted to sing in New York. Mr. Holland recognized her talent and encouraged her to follow her dream. He didn't know part of her dream was for him to go with her and have time to compose beautiful music. She knew he was married with a child. There were touching scenes about the tempting proposal but he didn't go with her to New York."

Sommer's expression revealed her thoughts—"So why are you telling me this movie story?"

Michael quickly read her thoughts and said, "That was preliminary to a similar story that really happened. But first, let me tell you what my dad said about people in this life. He said we want three things—pleasure, recognition, and security—in that order. He walked to his chair and positioned himself to look at Sommer. Her sad countenance caused him to hesitate before continuing.

"Okay, now my true story—My dad had a married friend in his late thirties who knew a girl half his age. They did leave for the bright lights of the city. Only this city was Nashville. He played the violin, or fiddle, and she sang."

Michael paused.

"This man told my dad that he couldn't fully explain or describe the rapturous feeling when she asked him to go with her. He said it was a chance of a life time. He further said the relationship was ecstatic bliss night and day, and he truly thought heaven was here on earth. He told my dad that when they were apart, even for an hour, he ached until she was in his arms again."

"Now Sommer, here's what I want to tell you."

He paused again and then went to her chair. On bended knees, he softly bared the pent-up throbbing in his heart.

"Sommer . . . Sommer, I love you. I do. I do love you. I ache when I'm away from you. I know you love me, and that makes my love for you and my devotion to you just so much deeper."

He encased her hands within his and spoke with even more affirmation.

"At times, I didn't think my heart would keep on beating until seeing you again. I don't want to eat. I sleep very little. Sommer, I'm in love with you bad—I mean good."

He smiled in spite of the seriousness of his words. Regardless of Sommer's melancholy for the pain she was imposing on the limp man before her, she managed a weak smile.

With more assertiveness than planned she replied to his declaration. "I understand, and I'm sorry. But let me tell you my side, and please try to understand what I'm up against. I can't be around your rich family and friends."

His mouth flew open. "WHAT! You mean . . . "

"I mean I don't belong in your world."

"Listen my dear, sweet Sommer. I want you to be with me—us together."

As if not hearing his last words, Sommer continued her side of the discussion.

"I could never be comfortable around your mother."

Another shriek from Michael. "That's not fair! You haven't met my mom. She is as nice and sweet as you. She would love and respect you.

Sommer seemed a bit jarred as a disturbing impression of what he must be thinking filled her mind. Neither spoke for a few anxious ticks of time. With gentleness Michael calmly remarked, "We could live in the house you're going to buy. We could make new friends. We could—"

"Michael! Are you hearing what you are saying? How long did your dad's friend stay in Nashville away from his family and friends?"

"They were together three months, living in a motel and eating in restaurants. His money ran out, and she started sleeping with an established Nashville musician."

"Well there you have it. It seemed they had pleasure aplenty for a while but no recognition or security. If we move in a small house in this town, you would keep your recognition as a successful business proprietor and of course have security with your bank account."

Before the stunned man could speak, a revived single mom had more to say.

"You would miss your family and friends and your Columbus town with all its familiar sights and sounds. And most importantly, you would miss the pleasure that you're use to because you would be unhappy living in an uncomfortable place. You would—"

In a leap, Michael jumped up and shouted, "Stop!" He marched to the fireplace in long strides and moved a crane so vigorously that two empty cast iron kettles crashed together with a loud clang.

Two really nice people, in a beautifully decorated spacious house, had some decisive thoughts to unravel before their conversation could continue. Michael stared at the cold fireplace and was tempted to bang the kettles together again. As he looked at the blacken bricks and stones, a warm, glowing fire paraded by his thoughts. He visualized a steaming kettle of vegetable soup and biscuits browning in the dutch oven. In a blink, the cold, dark fireplace was back in view. His shoulders were slumped, and his chin was almost on his chest. Spinning from a cheerless awareness was the fact that another dream was not going to happen.

He turned and asked his new but dearest love to forgive his outbursts, and then added, "I love you so very much I don't want to hurt you in any way."

"I'm sorry to have provoked you."

"But you're right, you know."

They looked deeply at each other for a long second.

"I'm going to leave now, but first may I tell you how I imagined our meeting today—especially after seeing you on the wall?"

Not giving her time to answer, he quickly said, "No, I should just go. No need to waste your time hearing about how a silly man's thoughts propelled him to believe that God actually spoke to him about . . . "

The dreamer stopped, and his shoulders slumped again as he looked at the floor. He then briskly walked toward the door and said, "Bye Sommer."

His hand was turning the knob when he heard, "Maybe it would help if you told me?" Her voice reflected a tenor that she was a little unsure of her essential reason for asking. Even so, the despondent, suntanned man on his way to his Columbus home town did not open the escape door.

He was realizing that love could be as powerful as a tree root in a rock crevice and can often move quicker and can be more destructive. His heart was shattered to the maximum extent possible while still providing life support. A major change occurred in his life today. He recently had been happily stepping on dream stones across an enchanted brook named love, but a minute ago he stepped onto a dry, uncertain future with no pleasant expectations. A shiver of hope quickened his senses, however, when she said, "Maybe it would help."

Sommer was still in the chair when he sat down. He wasn't sure the thrill of seeing her sitting on the wall could plausibly be reenacted after being drenched in the cold water of a second refusal. She patiently waited for some sounds from the man with his eyes closed. He didn't or couldn't look up as his lips begin to speak her name just above a whisper.

"Sommer . . . I . . . I doubt my being here today has made much difference to you. But—"

She bolted back with all the anguish her personality would allow. "Now wait a minute! It's my turn to say 'That's not fair.' This has been the most difficult day in my life. It is completely different from what I expected when I sat on the wall."

"Whoa! What did you expect when you said no to me for a second time?"

No answer came from a miserable girl about ready to cry.

"Okay, okay, I accept your answer and your reason. I don't agree, but I'm sure you thoroughly evaluated your position and believe it's the best way for you. Now, let me tell you how my day started."

He pressed the pause button to organize his thoughts before speaking.

"Remember what my dad's friend said about being away from his new young love?" He didn't wait for a reply. "I had been away from you for fourteen days—that's 336 hours. I awoke real early with you on my mind—in my mind and in my heart. I hadn't slept well but was energized and happy because I would be seeing you soon. Oh yes, I was aching, but it was gradually diminishing because at sixty miles per hour each mile would bring me one minute closer to you."

Slightly invigorated from early morning thoughts, he walked to the large window to the left of the fireplace. In a placid discourse, he described the initial moment when seeing her sitting on the wall (presently in his view). He told her the ache evaporated and was replaced with the immeasurable joy of believing they would today become a betrothed couple to be together always. This impression was based on the congeniality and enthusiasm conveyed in the phone conversation about the expensive rug. She was even bubblier during the second phone call about when he could see the decorated house.

When Michael turned from looking out the window, Sommer had pulled her legs under her and had curled in the chair. She looked more like a child than an adult.

He mentioned the kiss, and while remembering her soft warm lips, his heart almost exploded from an overload of joy. But as he remembered her negative response after the kiss, and his sickened heart made him dizzy. Before collapsing, he hurried to his club chair. Sommer had not spoken. Michael was silent while planning what to do next. One thing was for sure—leaving was going to be soon. But first, she should know a few more of his thoughts.

"Sommer, let me tell you some more of what I had hoped for today. I wanted to tell you that I wanted us to date a while before marrying. We could take some short trips, dine and dance, go to concerts, and did I say dine and dance? But then I want to always date you, or court as my grandfather used to say."

A more stabilized Michael Bentley turned and looked out the south-facing sliding glass door and pointed with his finger. "Right out there will be a Japanese Garden that we can plan together. I mean you can plan and I will help."

Still with his back to Sommer, he continued with a softness representative of his persona. "But most of all, I want to know and feel the thrill, the delight, the joy of holding you again after a short absence. I want the ache to melt when I see and hold you in my arms. And my dear, there's a difference between ache and pain because I also know how pain can pain."

"Please don't say any more."

"You're right. No need to say anything else because it seems nothing I say will make a difference with you."

He quickly turned and saw his beautiful, kindred-spirit friend more settled down in the chair with her hands over her ears. She couldn't understand why there were no tears. Before the full magnitude of his words could open the floodgates, Michael promptly said, "I'm sorry to be leaving under these circumstances, but I need to go. Good bye and good luck Sommer."

Michael again had his hand on the door knob when he stopped. Again, he aborted his exit.

"Oh, I almost forgot something. I meant to play a song."

He walked past Sommer and placed a CD on the entertainment cabinet. She seemed frightened and cringed in the chair showing no sign that she had reconsidered his proposal. He asked if she had seen the movie *The Great Caruso,* and she moved her head in a negative motion.

"It is a great movie that was released in 1951 and won an Oscar. One of the songs in the movie is famous. The music was written in the late 1800's by a full-blooded Indian from Mexico. His name was Rosas. I can't remember his first name, but anyway, he called it "Over The Waves." His tune was borrowed for the movie song with lyrics written by Paul Francis Webster. That's his song on the CD."

Michael had been looking at the girl he loved more than anything else in the world. It was going to take all his willpower to walk away without begging one more time.

"This Webster guy wrote lyrics for many great songs: "Secret Love," "Love is a Many Splendored Thing," "The Shadow of Your Smile," and "April Love." Michael moved toward the door with one last comment.

"Sommer," The man who had been rejected two times hesitated before continuing, "You know, I may write a song. I would title it 'On a Cloud.'"

Another pause before he spoke.

"My song would be based on . . . on" Michael looked out the window with his back to Sommer. "Okay, I have a beginning. Something like the times I've been in love. You know about Jodi and Kathleen. I've also been in love with three other girls. Each of them had me flying to different levels, but with you I've been on a cloud so high that I couldn't always see the ground."

He abruptly stopped talking and walked to the door. "Yes, I've been on a cloud. I've been on a very high cloud since meeting you. But right now, my feet are back on the ground heading for my Columbus town. Sell this house. I don't want to see it again."

The closing door was the catalyst that turned on the tears. She twisted and squirmed until she was soon lying in a fetal position. When the tears finally stopped, she inserted the CD and turned it off after Mario Lanza sang the second line.

> *When you are in love*
> *It's the loveliest night of the year*

For some reason she remembered playing Monopoly with her cousins what seemed like a hundred years ago. She had just finished playing a game and had lost everything because of a perception of not being worthy of Michael's family severed signals between her heart and mind. *She looked at the card in her hand that read: Advance token to your bedroom at home— do not pass go.*

Chapter Eleven

The last days of October were a blur. Sommer couldn't go to work during the remaining days of the week after Michael left. When she called the office, she had been crying so much that Alice thought she had a cold. Alice was excited and talked several minutes about meeting Jim Kelly. Sommer was jealous of her happiness and wanted off the phone to resume her crying.

November wasn't much different from the last miserable half of October. Some events occurred that had Miss Sad Rose bouncing from disappointments to frustrations to pity parties until the pain Michael mentioned was manifested in days and nights of lucid agony. In summary, it was a month of total unhappiness with one exception.

The wretchedness started early. On the first day of the month, Friday, John wrote a contract on the house she was going to buy. She had listed it the Thursday before Michael entered her life. She was involved with his decorating after receiving the Zliger house commission and didn't commit to purchasing her little house. Following the decorating, Michael left, and her heart and mind went on sick leave. All current actions and future plans were placed on hold. She would occasionally think about the house between crying sessions but would always decide to do the paper work later. She didn't think any more tears could flow after Michael left, but losing the house reopened the valve for many more.

The weather for November was generally nice with many sunny, fall days. The days just before and after Veterans' Day, however, were not at all nice and sunny. Eighty-three tornados ravaged parts of seventeen Mid-Atlantic States. There were a total of thirty-six deaths in five states with seventeen deaths in Tennessee. Seven people were killed in Morgan County—just two counties west from her county of Jefferson. The anxiety associated with rain, wind, and black skies had Sommer thinking about something else for a change.

There was no major damage in her community, but she was concerned about Michael's house. She had not been there since the day he left. While driving to the house, she finally decided that was twenty-two days ago. Another house item was also on her mind. She had not listed his house as he directed. Lately, she had been so confused and depressed that any credible logic and any consistent train of thought was not part of the Sommer who Michael loved. There was some kind of restraint that prevented her from listing the house. Something she didn't understand and couldn't rationalize in her mind. She intended to list it, and then when it was sold, a turbulent chapter of her life would be closed. Her mind of late had been gliding on a course with no destination or purpose. Only essentials were expended for minimal functions of daily life.

Everything outside the house looked okay except one tree limb was broken and a plastic bag was tangled in a shrub. After the door was opened, a blast of dizziness jarred her equilibrium as her eyes were clouded with tears of joy over the interior beauty. The exquisite furnishings and accessories had not been a part of her thoughts during the past three teary weeks. The coordinated colors and textures produced an artistic representation of gratification. She had to urge her mind to comprehend that all this balanced beauty was her handiwork.

Sommer stayed an hour. She dusted, made some minor rearrangements, and walked through the house remembering some of the last conversation with Michael. To her surprise, the house visit wasn't totally depressing, and her sorrowful state had not deepened.

She returned the following Wednesday to dust and, she secretly admitted, to admire. The passage of time had mitigated the sadness experienced the day Michael left. Pieces of her daily routine were slowly fitting back together.

Good fortune shone on Sommer the last Wednesday of November.She showed the Thompson house and wrote a contract for $300,000. The new owners were anxious for procession and closed two days later on Friday. The next day, Tim Bolling the mechanic, called and they had dinner together.

Sommer enjoyed being with Tim. He was a funny guy and made her laugh. She even went to church Sunday morning and sang in the choir. Sometime during the sermon, her mind wandered and she realized this was her first time in church since meeting Michael. Thinking of him prompted her now happy mind to remember she hadn't listed his house and that reminded her about the commission money she now had for her own house.

December was a really good month for Sommer. She listed another house and decided to buy it. But instead, she and Tim entered into a business venture—he persuaded her to loan him all her commission money to start his own used car business. In two or three months, she would have most of her money back plus receive ten percent interest on the balance. An invigorated Sommer skipped through the remaining December days with less and less thought of Michael. She had made a painful decision and Tim seemed the right choice. She wasn't completely beaming with lively enjoyment, but seeing Tim two times a week helped to forget the bridge she had tearfully burned. They discussed—or *he* discussed, his used car lot plans, and his excitement rolled over to Sommer until she was equally thrilled. He designed a sign:

CREEKSIDE CARS & TRUCKS
Start Rolling With Bolling

Buy Here—Pay Here
Tim Bolling—Owner

Tim bought four cars at an auction and sold the best one the first day to a friend on his bowling team. Three days later, his cousin bought the next best car. Sommer was pleased and completely comfortable with the loan. Feeling secure in a business deal should happen after a thorough background check had been completed. But Sommer didn't do this. So she didn't know that Tim had no credit and could not borrow from a bank.

The Christmas season was more happy than sad. The office party was a fun time, and she survived without Michael with less pain than expected.

The winter chill of January, for some unexplained reason, didn't seem all that bad, and days weren't totally boring. A simple routine was dutifully followed, which included seeing Tim one to two times a week. They didn't do anything different or exciting. By now she knew all his funny jokes, and his once amusing wit was becoming less humorous. But that caused no dreary impact on the summary of her usual sequence of activities. This was especially true toward the end of the month. Something was churning within her she couldn't explain. It was something delightful, or at least not gloomy. It seemed her emotions were splashing around, agitating strong feelings, and causing an inner disturbance she couldn't identify. In a flash, recognition came on the last day of the month—Friday.

The day started like many other recent days with no extremes. Most of the morning was spent in the office talking with Alice—to be more correct—*listening* to Alice. She and Jim Kelly were getting married in the summer. This bit of non surprising news didn't upset Sommer like it would have three months ago. For today she was feeling good about—well everything. Tomorrow, she would receive a really nice interest payment from Tim. It would be based on the entire amount of the loan because no principal had been returned. The interest would be for the months of November and December in 2002 and January 2003. He cited low sales due to cold weather as the reason for deferring the November and December payments.

Sommer had lunch with her mom and then drove to the house she wanted to buy. It had been on the market for nearly two months, and she believed Tim would soon come through with enough money for her to make the purchase. After an hour of planning and dreaming, she drove to Michael's house. It had been over a week since she was last there and had finally decided, just minutes ago, to list it when returning to the office. With the commission she could buy her house in case Tim didn't return enough of the principal for the down payment. As she unlocked the door, a satisfied feeling lightened her step over the threshold.

A familiar delight whisked before her dazzled eyes when she entered the house. The beauty of the room was consoling. During a slow, observant walk to the fireplace, another happy feeling was brewing within her. She couldn't put her finger on it but some excitement—some intensity mounting in a side road of her brain brought a smile. She remembered how Michael had been taken with the fireplace and cranes. He wanted meals cooked there like Rebecca Boone did it nearly 250 years ago. And then in a flash, she realized he wanted her to cook him meals using the pots and cranes.

A subsequent flash had the brilliance and force of a lightning bolt. To cook meals here, routinely, she should live here. Meaning, meaning—her face was suddenly on fire. She placed both hands on the stone front of the fireplace to keep from falling. Her legs were feeling like rubber so she pushed away and took four or five backward steps, until a sofa arm relieved the weight from her buckling legs. In a frame of mind blazing with wonderful expectations, Sommer Renée Rose fell backwards onto the sofa and shouted, "Yes." From a small section of her brain, she received instructions to whisper, "I would be his wife. I would be a Bentley." Before erratic breathing stopped altogether, "I would be one of them. I would be a Bentley and not have to measure up to their standards."

In slow, measured words, "I would be Mrs. Bentley. I would be a Bentley, and Michael said I would love his mother."

The impact of this revelation had no small effect on the limp form occupying the sofa. With a new set of goals and a new horizon to pursue, a dreamy Sommer Rose slid from the sofa to the floor. Still in an ecstatic state of shock, a fluffy mind coaxed anesthetized legs to let her stand. The next task for her less than coherent mind was to trounce the embarrassment for ever looking twice at Tim.

In a fairyland reverie, a Princess slowly walked through her palace admiring the splendor of the Bentley residence as a pleasant thought rambled through her jubilant mind. It will soon be under new management when Mr. and Mrs. Michael Bentley move in. The future Mrs. Sommer Bentley was so thrilled that she leaped with joy and for an instance thought she could fly like Tinkerbell.

Her new (to be) sparkling station in life suddenly dimmed when the flip side of her revelation registered. How stupid to resist the pleasure, recognition, and security when Michael first offered them. But she had been at the zenith of a glorious discovery trip, and it would take more than the remembrance of a foolish stubborn notion to bring her back to earth. She didn't recall leaving the house—oops—her palace. She drove home (her mother's house) in a daze. She would not write a listing today.

Lorrie Anne met her on the front porch.

"Mother, mother, you have a letter!"

Lorrie Anne was excited and further proclaimed, "It's from England can I have the stamp? Nanna said it might be from the Queen before she saw the return address name."

"Honey, I don't know anyone in England."

"Nanna said you know this man."

Sommer had the letter in her hand before entering the house. She indeed knew the sender and momentarily believed news within would only enforce or heighten her euphoric state of blissfulness.

Two hours later, still on cloud nine, Sommer settled on the back porch glider with a cup of herbal tea. Her refuge was most welcome this evening. She wanted to sit and joyfully recollect the glory of her revelation. After only a couple minutes, she remembered the letter.

Forgiven

A folded paper was inside the single, handwritten page.

January 23, 2003
Dear Sommer:

From the postmark, you can see I'm in England. The weather is worst than awful—not even close to the pleasant summer days I told you about. The sky is gray. Streets and buildings are gray, and people wear gray woolen clothing. I'm here because a prize Bentley car became available. It will be ready to ship in a few days.

I tried to write while in the states but would always tear up the letters. Not until this morning, could I finish a letter. I wanted you to read a poem about a dream I had last night. The dream was the most real, involuntarily episode in my life except the answered prayer I told you about what seems like years ago.

But my main reason for writing—I want to apologize for how I acted our last time together. I should not have just walked out. Many thoughts have troubled me about our last minutes together. Please forgive me for abruptly walking out of your life. I should have cordially wished you good luck and thanked you for the good times we enjoyed.

The letter was lowered and two moistened eyes stared out the window. A vision of her and Michael marching happily through life paraded past the grandstand of her mind. The tingling experienced after her revelation about becoming a Bentley was now amplified to a vibrant, pulsating, effervescent liveliness beyond belief. It took a while before eyes and mind could focus to finish the letter.

> *Well Sommer, when you read the poem, I guess the last two lines pretty well sum up the conclusion of our relationship—or I should say our acquaintance. Well maybe that isn't really correct. To be acquainted with someone is to know them less than intimately. But that's not right either. Some definitions of intimately are: closely, warmly, tenderly, and lovingly. At least for me, those four adverbs describe our ~~relationship~~—let me change that to our friendship.*

The single sheet of paper fell on her lap.

"Friendship!" raced through her now fluffy mind. The warm glow that surrounded her seconds before was now more like a north wind chilling her to despondency. But, nevertheless, the letter needed to be finished.

> *Well anyway, I'll always love you and know your memory will keep me warm when it's time for <u>my appointment beneath cold sod.</u>*

> *Well, that's it—when you sell my house, I'll sell the realty company and stay in Columbus or maybe move to England. Good luck and the best of togetherness to you and Tim.*

> *Thanks for decorating my house and for decorating my memory with pleasant dreams.*
> *Michael*

The poem would have to wait.

It was close to midnight when the letter insert was unfolded.

MY DREAM

I know I'll dream of you again
Like I did last night.
Again, I'll hold you close
Until dawn's first light.

You came to me with all your love
So happy were we.
Your touch was soft and warm
And so real to me.

You were mine last night
You were my love.
A gift supreme
From Heaven above.

Dreams of you will be sweet joy
'Til my life is through.
In peaceful sleep
I'll still dream of you.

First, it was numbness. No movement, no thoughts, no expectation of another breath, and no will to desire any of the above to ever happen again. A surrounding darkness and a deep grief swallowed up any prospect of a brighter future. Floodwaters of despair and desolation were rising and drowning her with intense physical pain and mental anguish. The line about good luck with Tim kept flashing before her bleary eyes. Then without warning, convulsions started. Her body was uncontrollably shaking, and heaving began before the sprint to the bathroom. Oh yes, then the tears—more than a river before a blessed period of rest started when her eyes closed.

Chapter Twelve

"Sommer! What's wrong? Is something wrong with your mother or Lorrie Anne?"

"No."

"Well what is it? You look like you've been rode hard and put up wet."

Indeed she did. Her sweater buttons and holes were misaligned and her black slacks were frosted with lint. Alice had never seen her hair so everywhere.

"I have lost Michael."

"I don't understand. You let him go weeks, months ago."

"Oh Alice, I'm so miserable. I don't know what to do."

"I'll tell what to do. First, sit down before you fall down."

Alice had been a second mother to Sommer and had willingly extended compassion and affection as if she were her own. The melancholy child before her looked more in need of assistance and support than at any other moment during their time together.

Between periods of crying and intervals of silence, required to stabilize breathing, Sommer recited the whole sequence of events leading up to the letter. The last scene at the house was particularly difficult to convey. Alice knew some of what had happened but now had the whole story. She looked intently at her sad friend with an expression that reflected, "I don't fully understand yet?" Before Sommer could cry again or again say her life was over, she handed the letter to Alice.

It was early Saturday morning, and no one else was in the office. Alice slowly read the letter and poem without distraction. When she addressed her forlorn friend, her comments were different than expected.

"From what I read my dear little girl, Michael believes he lost you to Tim but he still loves you—let me see, 'I'll always love you.' He even declares his love for you will continue while in his grave. I'd say it doesn't get more sincere than that."

A blank look from Sommer was the response Alice received for the interpreting of her friend's dilemma. Sommer walked to a window and gazed at the February bleakness until Alice summoned her to sit back down.

"But Alice, I said no two times to his proposal. When he left that last time, it was so final to me."

"Okay, but did you read his letter—I mean really read that he's sorry for . . . Oh Sommer, if you love him, like I think you do, tell him you want to be Mrs. Bentley. Tell him you're sorry to have been blind to his love and you will make it up to him by being the best wife in the world—or something like that."

After some hugging and tears from a different spring, gaiety filled the air. During the continuing festive conversation, a double marriage was even mentioned.

Sommer left and immediately came back in the office. She asked Alice for an advance. The blank look was now on Alice's face. She quickly recovered and stated, "What about your commission money?"

The happy Sommer of a minute ago cowered in fear of the forthcoming scolding from her second mother.

"What could you have spent it on? You haven't bought anything big that I know about."

She didn't get caught with her hand in the cookie jar, but an empty bank account was evidence that only crumbs remained after a stupid withdrawal. Alice listened with disbelief about the business deal with Tim.

"How much did you loan him?"

"All of it."

The glare of disapproval was a silent reprimand. An embarrassed Sommer didn't mention there was no interest payment today. The phone rang before the check was written. A young couple wanted to see the house Sommer had intended to buy for herself.

It was 2:00 p.m. when Michael's plane landed at the Columbus International Airport. He looked out the window at February bleakness. There was no one to meet him because he didn't tell anyone about his arrival, and there was no one to greet him at home because his mother was in Florida.

The England trip was definitely not much of a vacation—on a scale of . . . "Oh heck, what difference does it make. I got the car, and the nights at the pubs were happy periods of forgetfulness about the mess I have made of my life," he thought.

The wine he was sipping mellowed these thoughts as he sat alone at home. Last Christmas season, Nita invited (begged) him to come to her parents' home in Chillicothe, Ohio for an old fashion holiday dinner. That's when he took his first drink of wine. He and Nita then celebrated the birth of 2003 as they dined and danced to a new tune. Maybe it was the wine or the closeness of her or both—but Michael Thornton Bentley turned a page at 2am the first day of the New Year. Before recovering from his new reluctant commitment, he went to England and started drinking beer at the pubs.

Michael could never complain about Nita's love and devotion. She placed him above everything else. Everything—and often told him she would give him anything he wanted. She was an affectionate person and her attentiveness showed ample zeal and passion to please him. When together, she often anticipated his needs and desires and was quicker than "Radar" on the TV show *Mash* to please the man she loved.

It was she who asked Michael for his hand in marriage at the New Year's Eve party. He couldn't remember if he was in a stupor or in love but said yes. And in a few minutes, she would be walking through the front door to make a romantic dinner for two (her words). The door bell and the phone rang at the same time. He answered the phone and then opened the door.

"Hello.—Come in out of the cold."

"What do you mean Michael?"

He immediately and happily recognized the voice. "Oh . . . oh . . . I mean is it cold in Tennessee?"

"Well yes, but—"

Michael interrupted, "Just a minute."

During the lull, Sommer savored how she had unhurriedly anticipated saying how sorry she was for waiting so long before realizing how much she loved him and wanted to be his wife. She had even told Lorrie Anne that she would soon have a step father. An air of excitement stirred within the walls of her mother's small house. It would soon be official that Mrs. Sommer Bentley would be living in a big, big house.

"Did you sell my house?"

Sommer didn't answer. She was too enthralled with the prospect of her soon to be happiness to be surprised that he would question why she called. She also didn't know that her heart and soul swirling in an enchanted whirlwind of delight was heading for a hard landing.

"Did you call to tell me you sold my house?"

Before Sommer could answer, she heard a soft giggle that sounded like Nita his secretary.

If Michael could have seen the illuminated cheery color of her face change to pasty white he would have cried.

"No. No, but should be soon."

"You mean you have someone interested?"

"No. I mean warm weather will . . . " Sommer had to stop talking or she would bawl.

"Did you call to tell me the weather will be getting warmer?"

No answer from the Tennessee caller because she was distracted hearing Nita say, "Warm weather can't come soon enough to suit me."

With her last bit of composure, Sommer whispered, "I need to go now."

"Wait! Don't hang up. Did you get my letter?"

There was concern and compassion in his voice. The mistakes she had made with Michael were recycling in her throbbing head until she could barely hear his words. What could she tell Lorrie Anne?

With the tenderness of a baby cooing, Michael asked again if she received his letter.

"Yes."

Silence –

"Did you like the poem?"

"Yes."

Michael knew this wasn't the Sommer he still loved. Something was wrong with this conversation and he knew what to do.

"Thanks for calling and let's hope for warm weather. Goodbye."

"Bye."

Nita asked who called. After a vacant stare across the room, Michael answered with an inflection of pride, "My real estate agent in Tennessee . . . "

"Oh Michael! Are you going to sell your house?"

He said with assertiveness, "I might—it's on the market."

Michael had drunk too much wine to go dancing. So they merely circled through some unsteady dance movements in the living room, and Nita left earlier than intended.

"February, Oh where did thou goest?" chimed in the ears of a walking mummy. Valentine's Day was only remembered because Alice invited her to a party. She declined. The long, dreary days were absently navigated with no variance from meager essentials needed to maintain a semblance of living. The few smiles exhibited through the monotonous month were forced. The few joys—scratch that—there were zero joys in February. In Sommer's own words, "I have only one reason to live, and her name is Lorrie Anne."

The small house she once planned to buy sold right after the phone call with Michael when Nita was with him. Everything about Sommer's life began to be referenced before and after that pivotal phone call. Her next goal in life was Lorrie Anne's wedding day. The before pages were blurred from burning tears and are unreadable.

Oh yes, what about interest payments from Tim? The author wishes good news to report—but not so. Tim did sell some cars but reinvested the money by buying cheaper, high mileage cars and pickup trucks. He also hired a salesman to mind the lot while he spent his time in the repair shop. He had not kept his word on anything he agreed to over four months ago. Sommer

had not received a penny in returned principal or an interest payment since their verbal agreement. She was dreadfully depressed and getting desperate for cash flow. She could do nothing legal about the money from Tim because they had no signed terms and conditions. They hadn't talked for weeks.

Mothers are exemplary human beings. Their devotion to their children is commendable. Maybe it's because the baby is created over a nine month period that produces a special bond between mom and babe. There's a universal tenderness and affection emanating from the life giver to the helpless bundle of joy that connects them for life. Yep, mothers are extraordinary. Some children swear they have eyes in the back of their head.

Michael's mom was true to form. She knew that her son had been hurting about something since last October. She had several times asked if something was bothering him. There were never any in-depth discussions, but being a mother, she pieced together bits of conversation enough to know his source of pain was the Tennessee girl. She was concerned about his unhappy demeanor and greatly confused why he chose Nita to become his wife. She didn't completely dislike her, but she couldn't picture her son being fully happy with giggly Nita.

So what is a mother to do when she believes her son is slipping down a path to more sorrow than he is currently enduring? She picks up the phone and books a flight to Knoxville.

Michael read her note—Going back down south will call later about return date—with no undo concern.

Chapter Thirteen

The average March temperature for New Market, Tennessee is 45° with daily highs of 55°. Mrs. Naomi Bentley would enjoy 15° warmer days than her Columbus weather.

Naomi had twice talked briefly with Alice about Michael's business matters. Nothing was discussed about the relationship between Michael and Summer. A concerned mother, however, had all the missing bits and pieces about her hurting son and his Tennessee love after a long personal chat with Alice. The two new friends had lunch together and could hardly wait to initiate a plan of action they had conceived.

Sommer didn't come to the office the first two days in March. Alice had talked with her mother and knew there was no medical emergency. Sommer was in bed from a case of acute love sickness. In their conversation, Naomi had already told Alice that Michael did not go to the office yesterday. For their rescue plan to work, Alice had to get Sommer out of bed to show a house—the Bentley house.

Two hours later, Sommer was driving a nicely dressed lady to see a big house on a large lot with a beautiful view. Naomi remembered an excited Michael describing the house and view. There was only one house in the county fitting that description. The next one close was listed at $559,000 with a view of other nearby houses. Sommer had listed the furnished Serendip house at two million, and her passenger didn't change her facial expression when hearing the price.

Naomi Bentley was introduced to Sommer as Mrs. Thornton. She and Alice decided not to lie about her name but just not finish with saying Bentley. Mrs. Thornton Bentley's movements were graceful and lithe. Her willowy figure was a visual compliment to this disciplined, middle-age woman. Besides being pleasingly attractive, her mannerism reflected a distinctive quality of her character. There was spirit in her choice of words and her charming smile could cheer the gloomiest mood. Naomi's friends—old and new—enjoyed her company and always felt good to have been with such an eloquent lady. She was so refined yet unpretentious.

Before arriving at Michael's house, Sommer had already decided she liked this Mrs. Thornton, who insisted she be called Naomi. They talked about comfortable subjects that included the weather, the price of dairy products, new fashions, and the decline of song birds. Naomi also remarked about the tranquil atmosphere in this part of the Smokey Mountains. Sommer amended her observation by declaring a greater degree of peacefulness awaited her at the Bentley house. She didn't see Naomi's slight flinch when she heard Bentley. It seemed only natural when referring to the piece of real estate to show respect to the name of the owner. In Summer's mind, this was just one of the Oxford Realty houses for sale. The silly fantasy about living here was sent to the trash bin where impossible dreams are left to disintegrate.

Naomi reacted the same as Michael did when the driveway entrance arch came in to view.

"Oh please stop! That's beautiful. Oh my, have you noticed the sign—the words cut in the stones?"

A sickening feeling went all over Sommer as she remembered the same reaction from Michael. Before nauseating waves of dizziness completely short-circuited her mind, Naomi asked if she knew anything about Serindip? Lucky for Sommer the car was stopped. She could barely see the arch but knew (too well) the words cut in stone. Sommer's flat response was delivered in a whisper.

"I once knew but have forgotten."

"Oh my dear Sommer! How could you forget such a beautiful story about three princes of Serindip who found good by accident. It comes from a very old fairy tale written around 430 AD, based on the life of a Persian King. Facts have been embellished from folklore and translations through the many centuries, but the story begins when the King sends forth his three sons from their kingdom to acquire a broader education. The most familiar fable translated into English is about the three princes searching for an imaginary camel blinded in one eye. They had an uncanny ability to find good by accident."

While Naomi took a breath, Sommer seemingly remembered about the sign. She spoke with hesitation. "I thought an . . . an Englishman . . . Wal . . . Walpole . . . wrote—"

"Oh yes! Hoarse Walpole, third Earl of, I think of Oxford. He was an author but didn't write The Three Princes of Serindip. He coined the word 'serendipity' when writing about the three princes in one of the many letters he wrote. I happen to know about Serindip because each week when we play bridge, we discuss some topic we consider interesting."

Naomi smiled as they admiringly looked at the inscription on the arch—one for a more detailed history of the word and the other because her son had mentioned his good luck for finding the word obscured by a tangle of vines.

Naomi's breathing became erratic as they drove along the winding driveway lined on both sides with large, white pine trees. The invigorating drive was about the length of a football field. When they parked, her breathing became more irregular as the beauty and size of the house filled her eyes.

"Ahhhh Sommer, this is truly a king's palace. Someone with loving imagination built this for some special reason."

"I just recently found out that the builder was a retired NASA engineer. He built it for his wife as a surprise fiftieth wedding anniversary present. She stayed in Florida until it was finished. Their name was Zilgler. They had lived here less than five years when she died."

While they were getting out of the car, Sommer remembered that Michael was going to surprise his wife (to be). Naomi asked why the house was for sale before remembering she knew. Despondency was already surging through Sommer for thinking of Michael, and the question almost brought tears. This lady seemed like she could afford the house, so the commission carrot stopped the tears.

"The ma . . . the person de . . . decided to . . . "

"Did he change his mind about living here?"

"Yes. Yes, that's right."

If Sommer detected the 'did he change . . . ' it didn't show.

"This is truly a mansion. I like what I've seen so far."

The real estate agent wasn't emotionally able to go inside, so she led the prospective buyer into the front yard. It didn't help a bit to ease the sudden pangs of pain that were affecting her ability to concentrate as almost every accolade and praise that had come from Michael was coming from Naomi. They didn't sit on the wall but did linger to enjoy the peacefulness and the rhythmic murmur of the stream.

Inside, Naomi apologized for being so excited with her initial outburst when seeing the beauty of the furnishings. She then silently and slowly walked around the first floor, ending at the fireplace. After a brief glance at the kitchen, she walked to the back of the room and placed a hand on the baby grand piano. Sommer was looking out the sliding glass door when Naomi spoke in a rising intonation, "I can't imagine why someone would want to sell this beautifully decorated house."

As those words registered, Sommer closed her eyes, and in a flashing mirage, saw details of a Japanese Garden in the side yard. The illusion only lasted a second but long enough to painfully remember when Michael stood here and visualized her dream garden. She was jarred back to a more realistic picture when she turned as Naomi spoke.

"I want to know who decorated this palace. I can't believe that just one person could do such a superb coordination of hues and textures. And the perception of size and shape of furnishings with respect to volume of space on this first floor is most commendable. And Sommer, the large Persian area rug is the most exquisite one I have ever seen. It is the exact one for the room, especially with the two facing leather sofas and the long narrow table. And there in the corner by the window area, he, or they, tastefully placed a granny apple green and sunshine yellow ice cream table and chairs. It is just the right percentage of splash to excite the eye after the balanced earth tone colors elsewhere in the room. They have thoughtfully designed many conversation areas throughout, including the ten place dining table and the eight place wicker table in the sun room. Oh yes, the pecan card table near the piano and, of course, the sofas and club chairs."

Naomi stopped a minute to catch her breath. Sommer was either stunned to numbness or ready to faint. She was trying to decide which when Naomi stated that she wanted her house in Ohio redecorated by the ones who decorated this house.

She screamed when Sommer collapsed in a club chair.

Fifteen minutes later, they were enjoying a cup of tea. One had revealed her love for Michael and the other had confessed why she was looking at the house. Sommer was stunned beyond words. The letter and poem sent from England were about his love for her, but to also hear about a mother's observation was ample reason to rejoice. And in addition to this good news, Michael's mother was no one to dread; Sommer liked her immediately.

Chapter Fourteen

Sommer had never before made a decision so fast. The sounds, scent, and comfort of the airplane wrapped around her like a warm blanket. She was accompanying Naomi Bentley to Columbus, Ohio to do some interior decorating. But the thrill of decorating wasn't foremost in her thoughts. A certain pre-fixed notion in her mind had happily evaporated and a certain suntanned young man would soon be her husband. It would happen because she would beg forgiveness, on her knees, for rejecting him two times. Her future mother-in-law, by her side, couldn't reach Michael by phone, but a glorious reunion was just a few air miles away.

Naomi's house in suburban Columbus was empty. Michael's new secretary, Amber, didn't know where he was. She told Naomi he had not been in the office today and had not called. The whereabouts of Michael was solved at 4:00 p.m. when Sommer called Alice. She and the lost boy had just finished twenty minutes of confessions. Alice told her part in getting 'Mrs. Thornton' to meet Sommer, and Michael sobbingly declared his love for Sommer. While wiping her tears from a beaming smile, Alice handed the phone to a man in love with a girl sent to him from God.

The man said hello without enthusiasm.

The girl gasped as she blurted, "Michael! You . . . you are down there?"

"Where are you?"

"Up here."

"Where?"

"At your mother's house."

"What . . . what are you doing there? Why are you there?"

"I came here to see you."

"I came to Tennessee to see you."

Michael absently and confusingly informed Alice.

"She's in Ohio."

A pleasing smile was her reply.

Both players in this love game had absolutely decided that yes, yes, yes they would unite for life. They talked for a few more minutes. Sommer more fully explained why she was up north, and Michael confessed he had to go south to see her one more time before moving to England.

When Michael entered the room, he heard classical music and then saw her near the dining room French doors—a reminiscent flash from the day he met Jodi when he was seventeen. Summer didn't move, and Michael didn't move. It was like they were seeing each other for the first time. They seemed to be waiting for some facet of the past to validate that this really was the moment to begin the rest of their lives (together).

The embrace was more spiritual than carnal—the closeness and the warmth—the uncluttered knowledge that this reunion was to continue forever. A mutually desired kiss sealed the contract. There were no obstructions or restraints to compromise the designed effect of lips transmitting true intentions from heart to heart. The Recording Angel, however, most likely smiled as a score was posted because the embrace fetched a higher mark than the kiss.

Standing in the middle of the room with outstretched arms holding hands, Michael softy spoke.

"Do you remember I once said I wanted to feel the thrill of holding you after a short absence?"

Sommer's head was slightly tilted and lowered. Her acknowledgement could be seen in her moist eyes.

"I wanted the ache of missing you to melt while holding you."

Another embrace double tied their love knot to ensure the strains of life couldn't pull it asunder.

Michael suddenly looked serious but delighted at the same time.

"Do you remember anything else I said the last time at the house?"

"Please Michael—that was my most painful day ever."

"No, no, not that part. That was my most painful day also. I mean some of the things I wanted us to do before we marry."

His delightfully serious expression changed to a solemn look deeper than just a somber veneer.

"By the way, will you mar—?"

"YES! Yes, Yes."

Dear reader, you reckon the Recording Angel noted the radiant smile on Michael's happy face?

"Good!"

They were still standing holding hands and adjusting to their new station by enjoying the thumping of their hearts.

"I meant about dining and dancing and concerts and . . . " Michael looked to the far corner of the room and spoke as if in a trance.

"Sometime, I want us to rendezvous someplace like under the big clock at the train station and pretend we have been apart days instead of minutes or hours. I want to repeatedly rejoice from the thrill of holding you again and again. My dear Sommer, would you—could we have a date tonight? I know a lovely place to dine and dance.

Michael Thornton Bentley was beginning a relationship with Sommer unlike most others in current society. Her devotion and faithfulness to him would be openly manifested as she respectfully gave her unabridged love in attitude and behavior.

Chapter Fifteen

Sommer happily, joyously, cheerfully, and blissfully spent the remaining days of March in Ohio with her Prince Charming. Affable hours of dining, dancing, sightseeing, and planning their future passed in a whirl of thankfulness. They gave God all the credit for their happiness.

Michael spent most of April in Tennessee. He stayed in his house and two happy people spent hours together each day. A landscape architect was commissioned to design the Japanese Garden. Sommer and the architect worked closely together so the finished project would be exactly as she had so often dreamed.

Construction of the dream garden began during the first week of May. The excitement level soared at Serenidip. Sights and sounds had Sommer's pleasure glands overly stimulated until she would momentarily forget about the man making all this possible. By the end of the second week in May, the pond was finished waiting for rain. The moon bridge was nearly completed. Also, during the second week of May, Michael bought a tractor, a trailer, and a chainsaw. He tirelessly cut firewood from trees removed during the pond construction.

When Sommer took time to perceptively place activities in order, a void or a missing link would leave her uneasy about the immediate future. Marriage had been discussed with specifics, but she had no engagement ring. The wedding would be at Serendip, and they would honeymoon in England. She wanted to show her ring to friends—well, anyone who cared to look. Alice had a large rock she was eager to flash and show. The lack of a ring was on Sommer's mind more than maybe it should have been, and she would feel ungrateful when it surfaced. Her thoughts of being denied a ring always recalled the fact that Michael had been quick to give Kathleen a ring (which she did not return). Nevertheless, Sommer was happy and fervently extended passionate enthusiasm and devotion to the man she would love forever. After each pity party, however, she would feel ashamed and would hold her man a little tighter.

Michael and Sommer often had lunch at the wall. Well-appointed outdoor furniture greatly enhanced the tranquility of Michael's favorite outside place at Serendip. Sommer had arrived early this beautiful May day. She had spent most of time at the garden site so lunch was simple—pimento cheese spread on dark rye bread, chips, peppermint tea and lemon pound cake. After lunch and after the serenity of Michael's favorite place infused a second helping of contentment in their minds and hearts, he announced that his desire was to have supper prepared at the fireplace. The announcement was not a surprise. Sommer smiled and told her pioneer prince the menu was in her pocket. She knew all the firewood cutting was for this reason. She even had a whimsical notion he would wear a Dan'l Boone deerskin outfit for supper.

Sometimes in a person's life, a special dream really comes true. Two young people in love sat at the card table drenched with the glow of the big fireplace. It was Sommer, however, who was attired in period dress. When she went home to get her mother to help pick wild greens, she changed clothes to resemble Rebecca Boone. The workers at the Japanese garden site must have been amused seeing her picking the same wild plants people gathered for food nearly 250 years ago.

A man at Sommer's church had a small out building used for processing deer meat. He and hunter friends would gather to change field dressed deer into packets of deer steaks. The friends worked assembly line fashion to remove all tendons and ligaments (removes wild taste) and then the red meat was cut into two inch squares. The squares were machine tenderized and packed into ziplock bags ready for the freezer. Sommer had killed some of the deer and had worked and fellowshipped with the other hunters. A package of venison steaks would be used for her pioneer supper that also included wild greens, pickled beets (from her mother's cellar), mashed potatoes, gravy, biscuits, tea and a surprise dessert.

Yes, special dreams do come true. Michael was impressed and awed and nearly overcome with joy and admiration for Sommer when he viewed the colorful presentation of the pioneer meal. She had borrowed two pewter place settings from her mother to better authenticate a typical meal cooked at an open fireplace. Earlier she had made a rhubarb sauce at her mother's house and placed it in hot coals. This sauce over a buttered biscuit was the surprise dessert—a favorite in Daniel Boone's time. The home-made butter came from an Amish family.

The meal, wrapped in nostalgic echoes of a long ago rustic time, was much more than Michael had expected. Two thankful people in love pensively watched dancing flames and were lost to the present. Reflective thoughts of the meal and a simpler time had them overflowing with contentment. They were living moments many people never get a chance to enjoy. Just before another twisted yellow flame totally hypnotized Michael, his eighteenth century dressed friend began clearing the table. The cast iron tea kettle softly spewed steam as if indicating it was time for another cup.

A calming ambiance in the fairyland room had been filling their hearts with delight until they both knew Heaven was only an embrace away. To assuage the urge to fly, Sommer sat down and they slowly and dreamily sipped their tea. Michael rapidly searched his memory for the right poem from the masters to describe the pleasant flickering glow on Sommer's beautiful homespun face. Before the poetic stimulus of this poignant moment escaped up the chimney, he recited two lines he had penned just last night.

> *"Meaningful moments I hold dear*
> *Only happen when you are near."*

Sommer sat motionless with an endearing affection for the wonderful man near her. She tried to speak but could only transmit through moistened eyes all the fondness in her heart that had been compounding since she confessed her love for him. Their smiles and eye contact were whispering a thousand words a second.

Michael had been anxiously waiting for the perfect and meaningful moment to give her an engagement ring. He was presently inhaling the sweetness of that 'just right' instant. But first, a short prologue to explain the delay seemed in order. He seriously spoke.

"Sommer."

She had drifted into pleasant thoughts and was startled by his voice.

"Oh! Oh yes—What is it?"

"Do you remember when I told you about my father buying the cars in England?"

"Yes, and you went with him I think five times."

"That's right and my Uncle Chance and Aunt Ida went with dad and mother one time. Aunt Ida, my mother's youngest sister, fell in love with the Jaguar dad bought on that trip. She couldn't afford it and through the years would often mention it should be willed to her. Okay, the reason I'm telling you this is because my grandmother Edith gave her engagement ring to Aunt Ida."

Michael stopped for any reaction. Sommer blankly stared with a puzzled expression. He quickly continued, "I wanted you to have grandmother's ring."

Sommer's expression changed to a look of gratitude. She had a notion to put forth her left hand to receive it because Ida's son Robert (of Cedar Point trip) was already married. Michael's next words changed gratitude to disappointment.

"She wouldn't give it to me."

Before the lovely person in his view could totally react in the negative, he smiled and said, "But I finally got it for you."

While retrieving the ring from his pocket, Sommer asked, "How did you get the ring?"

"I traded for it."

"What . . . what did you trade?"

"In the beginning, she refused to give it up until I offered the Jaguar."

"You what?"

"It's not a big stone, but I had no choice."

"You mean you . . . "

"Yep."

"Oh Michael, you are so . . . oh Michael I don't . . . "

"Don't say it. I love you a million times more than that old Jag."

Since Sommer met Michael, she had been many times vaulted to regions of delight never before even vaguely considered. She was looking through the Milky Way when seeing the ring. The tears started as she actually climbed across the table to fling her arms around the man she loved. Her intention was so aggressive that his chair tipped backward and Sommer slid down on him as he slammed to the floor. The engagement was celebrated with giggling, crying, and kissing after neither reported any injuries.

Grandma's ring was indeed small—a one-eighth carat solitaire. But Sommer's ring was not small at all. Michael's design included the small stone and mounting surrounded with six half carat pear shaped diamonds. When Sommer could intelligently speak again, she gasped and said, "That's over three carats."

It was May the twenty-third, and on this glorious Friday evening some passionate, serious thoughts were entertained about moving the wedding day forward or . . . but no, they would wait.

Sommer drove home on a cloud so high and so removed from earthly things, that she was blissfully ignorant of what would happen two weeks hence.

Chapter Sixteen

When Michael was certain he would soon marry, he petitioned the court for visiting rights with his son. By a prearranged agreement, on June the sixth, Jodi and Adam arrived at Serendip. Sommer was there and painfully saw the beauty of Adam's trim mother. Michael had met her at the airport. She came with Adam to see for herself where he would be visiting.

Michael had not seen Jodi since their idyllic day at Cedar Point seven years ago. Visitation negotiations were conducted by lawyers. The two brief times he had seen Adam were at Aunt Flo's in Sandusky, Ohio. Jodi was down the street at her Aunt Rachel Buckenberger's house. Michael had occasionally wondered why Jodi didn't want to see him, but didn't allow the mystery to interfere with his seven years of living up to now. Which brought him to the now.

They had an amiable conversation while driving from the airport. Her mother died last year, and since that time she had been working at the Gary, Indiana City Court House. Her truck driving boyfriend moved in with her after she inherited her mother's house. She knew Michael was recently engaged but no engagement seemed to be in her future.

For nearly an hour, Michael showed his guest the house and grounds. Sommer managed to elude Jodi by exiting through the garage and losing herself in the Japanese Garden. She was reluctant to admit a wave of jealousy had her more than a little upset. After Michael and Jodi lingered (too long) at the wall, Sommer's dismay changed to seething distrust. She had, by now, profiled Miss Jodi Moss. To begin, her tight, red dress couldn't be comfortable traveling attire. Sommer believed Jodi knew exactly the type of house Michael owned and didn't need to check if it was suitable for Adam to visit. Sommer further believed Miss overdressed, concerned mother was here to let Michael know she was now ready to be his wife and live in this big beautiful house. Sommer surreptitiously walked in the garden watching Michael talking to that Jezebel. Each sound of laughter raised the level of her suspicion until pent-up anger boiled into a furiously jealous rage. All of this was doubly disturbing because fury was not representative of Sommer's serene personality. She managed to stay hidden in the Japanese Garden until Michael left with Jodi and Adam for the motel. When Michael returned, she was gone but had left a note stating she was preparing dinner for him at her mother's house.

She had timed it almost to the minute when the phone rang.

"Hi Sommer. I was planning to . . . "

Sommer interrupted. She knew exactly that he was planning to dine with Jodi and Adam. Blithely, she presented what she was planning.

"Michael, I'm fixing one of your favorite meals. It will be ready in thirty or forty minutes. Then after dinner, we need to go over our guest list again."

"Can't that wait 'til tomorrow?"

"Of course, but I would like to finalize the list as soon as possible."

Michael hesitated before agreeing to be there in thirty minutes. Sommer was uncomfortable with being so pushy, but she believed Jodi was a real threat. That gold digger was not going to take her man. Sommer admitted she had been reluctant to stake her claim but three sparkling carats were proof that her entitlement was duly registered.

There was no effervescence in the conversation during the meal except for Lorrie Ann's excitement about meeting Adam. The woman in red flew into town making Michael and Sommer's relationship a little strained. Sommer didn't ask what he told Jodi about not dining with her. He was obviously upset because of the changed plans. Michael spent an apprehensive hour after dinner and then abruptly left. The tenseness in his goodbye embrace lingered in Sommer's thoughts as she sat on the back porch contemplating a defense to keep Michael out of Jodi's greedy arms.

Adam was to spend the last two weeks of July with his dad, even though the marriage would not be until Friday evening the eighth of August. The newlywed couple would then leave for England the following Tuesday.

Marriage plans were more extravagant than Sommer had originally planned. She had envisioned being married on the moon bridge with a reception following in the house. Michael wanted an outside party venue in a large tent containing a dance floor, live band, lights and more lights. He envisioned it extending into the night. When his and Kathleen's engagement was announced, the pomp and pageantry was impressive. But

Michael wanted his own wedding to be so spectacular that it would be enjoyed and remembered as the best ever held in the county.

Michael was making all necessary arrangements and pieces of the (his) party plan were interlocking smoothing into the big picture. Sommer was mostly going with the flow—true to his personality, he was in charge. They would have discussions, but Michael's master plan didn't appreciably change. Sommer was by no means dismayed. This was the happiest time in her life. Dreams she had never imagined were unfolding as enchantingly as a caterpillar changing into a butterfly. There was only one smudge in her new world of glitter. Jodi Moss was an unwelcome cloud, and it had been really painful to have Michael show *her* house to this unsolicited stranger.

Jodi and Adam would leave Sunday. Michael insisted that Saturday would be family day. He was anxious to connect with his son. His plan was to have breakfast with Jodi and Adam. The four would then have lunch at Serendip. Michael and Adam would hike down to the stream below the wall. This part of his plan was not to Sommer's liking since she and Jodi would be left together.

Sommer decided to be a gracious but assertive host. She told Jodi that Michael bought the house for his fiancée and then changed his mind and was going to sell it if she didn't marry him. She talked some about the decorating. The checking account in her name was mentioned with a guise that she was trusted with a very large amount of money after Michael had known her only three days. Sommer thought Miss Tight Jean Lady should know from this that Michael was off limits. She thought at times her dynamic behavior was a bit overdone, but no one was going to steal her Prince Charming. She had cried and hurt too much for Jodi to waltz into their lives and painlessly take the blue ribbon.

The sightseeing and dinner in Knoxville was almost more than Sommer could endure. It was not apparent to her if Michael detected her discomfort. He was (she guessed) trying to make up for lost time with Adam, and her uneasiness was well concealed. The only good part of the trip was the way Michael looked at her—repeatedly. Her solid butternut dress wasn't tight fitting, but the slash around her small waist revealed her ample curves. At the end of the day, Jodi no longer seemed a threat to a happy life with Michael.

The five weeks between the weekend Jodi and Adam visited and when he arrived, middle of July, zipped by quickly for Sommer. Some type of marriage detail needed to be dealt with every day. In addition, her excitement level seemed to double each passing day. Alice and Jim Kelly were recently married, and their happiness made Sommer all the more eager to join the ranks of blissful togetherness.

Two weeks before Adam arrived, Michael was in Columbus. He was leaving from there to pick up Adam. Jodi had insisted that Adam not travel alone.

Adam was a well mannered child but he had not inherited Michael's ebullient personality. He was more reserved in his conversation and actions. All the people around him were new to him including his dad. There were times, however, when he was relaxed and meshed with the adult talking and joking. After a week, he and Sommer were getting along much better than she had expected. Michael was elated with his fast track father-son relationship. With the exception of some menu adjustments, the three were having an enjoyable time together. After a slow, shy start, Adam and Lorri Anne became genial playmates.

Michael was opening an office in Knoxville and went there the second Monday morning of Adam's visit. Sommer, Adam and Lorri Anne had a picnic lunch at the wall. They were ready to leave when Sommer made a casual comment about still wrestling with the wedding guest list. Adam promptly remarked with a statement that changed the peacefulness of the afternoon to the most turbulent moment in her life. She had experienced many disappointments and surprises in her twenty-four years, but nothing had ever affected her like the consequential words Adam casually spoke.

"My mother and father like to wrestle."

In an instance, Michael's unnatural and blank stares the past week whirled in her numbed mind. He at times seemed to be thinking about something different than the subject of the real-time circumstances. Sommer's face was flushed from the apprehension of what this could mean. She could only manage one word.

"Oh?"

The nuance in her single word didn't register with Adam to offer more details. She did not really want to pry, but alleged implications to her future required more information.

"Adam."

A pang of meddling guilt prevented her from finishing her inquiry, but the consequences were too important not to continue.

"You say your mother and father like to wrestle?"

Michael and Adam were a day late getting to Serendip because Adam was too sick to leave when Michael arrived at Jodi's house. He spent the night with his son and a woman he once wanted to marry.

"Yes, I saw them. Father stayed at our house when he came to pick me up. He slept in Uncle Teddy's room. After I went to sleep, mommy was making a noise that woke me."

Adam had apparently expounded sufficiently and asked Lorri Anne to race with him to the house. Sommer cleared her throat and quickly asked, "Did you say he spent the night at your house?"

"Yes."

Sommer had to have more—being respectful to a private event no longer mattered.

"Well Adam, did you watch your parents wrestle? I mean . . . did you watch them very long?"

"I saw them when the noise woke me at night and then mommy woke me again in the morning with the same noise. I asked if they liked to wrestle, and both of them said yes."

Sommer couldn't stand and could barely breathe. She told them to go race. Her world was upside down and her Prince Charming was disappearing as had happened in the cloud formations. She could not have been any more devastated had she known more about the wrestling matches.

Jodi had feigned Adam's sickness to compel Michael to spend the night. Her live-in truck driver friend, Ted, was two days out on a six day run. Jodi and Michael drank wine and danced after Adam was sent to his bedroom early. She played a trump card on Michael's male persona that Sommer had not and would not have done before being married. Jodi came to his room wearing only a robe, and informed him that she knew he wanted her. While removing the robe, she added, "Again." Sommer also did not know Adam was sent to a friend's house after breakfast with instructions to play two hours.

The news and imminent ending of happy dreams happened so excruciatingly fast that Sommer's sudden headache and nausea caused her to lose her lunch. She didn't remember what she did until Michael returned, but immediately announced that she and Lorrie Anne needed to leave. Getting out of his sight was her first priority. If she gave a reason for leaving so quickly again, she couldn't remember. If he was alarmed with her hurried departure—she didn't care.

Michael had changed her life. Before meeting him, she was content with marginal happiness and had a tender, careful attitude. She was now an angry person. He lovingly persuaded her to seize the impossible dream and step into the future with confidence. The same Michael had now made her enraged and transformed her empathetic approach in life to an "I don't care way of thinking."

Chapter Seventeen

It had been a long time since Sommer was on a bus. Leaving Tennessee was an easy decision. She had never been so sure of anything before. A new place with new people to reprogram her mind seemed the proper thing to do. After leaving that big house, it only took two days to make exit arrangements. Putting the ring in an envelope with a one sentence note was surprisingly painless. She earlier thought actually giving up the ring would bring a flood of memories and an ache she once heard could even cause a change of mind. Alice was to give the note to Michael. Sommer asked her to read it and then told her the rest of the story. She tried to get Sommer to reconsider. After a tearful parting, Alice read the note again.

Good luck with your wrestling career.

There was no salutation nor was it signed.

Lorrie Anne was asleep when the bus crossed the West Virginia state line. Plans were to stay with a cousin, Freddie Jo, who lived in Ona, a small community fifteen miles east of Huntington, West Virginia. Freddie Jo was delighted to help Sommer. The two had not been together for five years, so some catching up was in order. A week after arriving, Sommer had a job at the nearby mall. An aunt who lived five minutes from Freddie Jo agreed to babysit Lorrie Anne and let Sommer use her car.

In an amazingly short time, her life was moving toward normalcy. Lingering effects of the roller coaster ride with Michael were abating more each day. She was making new friends at work and at the Beulah Ann Baptist Church. The church family made her feel comfortable, which was a giant step to forgetting the reason West Virginia was her new home. She became active in work with the church youth and was well received and loved by all. She became an instant celebrity after winning a horse shoe pitching contest at the annual Homecoming Reunion. In September, she moved her membership to Beulah Ann.

One bright, autumn morning, she realized it was October. A year ago she met a man. They exchanged some personal information that began a relationship destined to bond them for life and forever. The splash of fall colors, in her view, was not appreciably different from those she enjoyed with this man in Tennessee. She had not intently thought about Michael or Tennessee since the check arrived from his attorney. When he learned from Alice about Sommer's loan to Tim Bolling, Michael sent his attorney to Tennessee. Tim was informed that his property had enough environmental infractions that County, State, and Federal fines would force him to sell everything— plus he would probably spend some jail time. This may not have all been true, but Tim knew the septic tank had a problem. In short, the attorney arranged for an absolute auction to retrieve Sommer's money.

Contented days of October drifted by on warm winds that had Sommer believing a new beginning was possible. West Virginia events and passage of time had mellowed her thoughts to only occasional reminiscent scenes of the happiest and saddest time in her Tennessee life.

There had been no direct contact with Michael. Alice said he cried tears of regret when he picked up the ring in late June. She also informed Sommer he came in the office two weeks later to list his house, and she and Jim bought the realty company.

In the midst of her recovering period, another problem or concern prompted some serious consideration of her immediate future. A nice man from the church had asked her for a date. They had been together in a group, and she liked him but was not ready to walk off the moon bridge into a misty shroud of uncertainty. They could probably enjoy some happy times, but she could never survive the grief if new dreams were to crumble.

November was nearly over before Sommer said yes to the date. He was kind and considerate, and she often caught herself comparing him to Michael. On the third date, she told him why she came to West Virginia and asked him to forgive her for encouraging a friendship without her full commitment. They continued to sit together at church.

December 2003 began with happy thoughts of Christmas and family time. Sommer's mother was coming to spend some time with her sister. Seasonal gaiety was in hearts and in your face at the mall ten miles from West Virginia's second largest city, Huntington. Sommer was working overtime, which gave her less time to think about a certain subject. Michael's house had not sold, and Alice had no other news when she last made her weekly call.

Cold wind, ice, and snow in West Virginia were not much different from the Tennessee variety. Sommer had never worked at a mall and had never routinely negotiated a large, icy parking lot. She knew about black ice but failed to notice a small area of it as she was hurrying to work one cold morning. She was thinking about her mother who was arriving later that day. In an unfortunate second, she slipped, and her head hit the concrete pier of a parking lot light pole. Paramedics responded quickly, and she was rushed to St. Mary's Hospital in Huntington.

The mall office called the next of kin, but her mother was not at home. Her cousin was then notified. She immediately called Alice who called Michael. He was in Columbus and was at the hospital three and a half hours later.

When Michael entered the hospital three dreary days ago, he was confidently hopeful of a speedy recovery. When engaged seven months ago to the only girl he ever truly loved, he was fully satisfied in his heart and mind that his most special prayer request had been answered. The assurance of his prayer application being answered was so spiritual and so absolute that he considered it a covenant with God. He believed then a happy marriage was in his future. Well, the future was here, and his foolish heart sent that happy marriage to it never will happen land.

He could no longer rationally think or reason. He was tired, hungry, and needed a bath. He had sat for minutes with his throbbing head cradled in his hands.

Outside, nearly horizontal sheets of rain were like a huge, translucent mantle making all objects blurry. Then the December winds suddenly intensified, and rain changed to sleet. In waves of hammering fury, frozen ice pellets bounced off the window glass. Each volley was like a thousand darts piercing his heart—an apathetic heart—but not totally listless and numb.

He could still feel pain. After the first day in the hospital, his strength had been waning. Now, every resolve in his life was disappearing. His will—his strong determination to keep fighting, grasping, and clawing for another forward inch was gone. No more reserve energy. His tank was empty. As her life was ending—so was his. He was not going to get the chance to beg her to forgive him.

Pinging pellets were echoing inside an empty body shell that once was filled with overflowing happiness. Michael Bentley had been on a cloud so serene that anything contrary was out of sight. He had no knack on his own for finding good by accident, but with God's help he had held his "serendipity" in his arms. She was the epitome of goodness who had vaulted him to joyous heights. Her smile, her honesty, her candor in conversation, her compassion and her unmitigated love for him was to be no more. There would be no more pleading and begging for an answer to "Why?" Why did he step over the line with Jodi? That nightmarish thought was constantly on his mind the past three days. Sometime in the wee hours last night, he wrote a poem. He didn't know why, but he was going to leave it on her bed after saying a last goodbye. In an involuntary reflex, he slowly unfolded the sheet of paper and again read the saddest lines he ever wrote.

FOOLISH HEART
It's not the same heart beating when you were mine.
I am shamed and sorry since I crossed the line.
Tonight I'm praying come back to me.
Oh dear Lord please, please hear my plea.

I would give half of my tomorrows for just one yesterday
That sad day my foolish heart went astray.
I would give half of my tomorrows to hold you one more time
To hold you and know again you are mine.

The gray sky had turned as deep black as his foreboding mood. A whorl of shadows filled Michael's brain, except for one small sane part telling him not to be present when the final curtain came down. He said goodbye to the only person who ever really mattered to him. He knew without a doubt that God forgave him, for sinning when he was seventeen years old. Sleeping with Jodi last summer was so humiliating and disrespectful to Sommer that he couldn't believe God would ever forgive him. When he kissed her cheek, he had a warm feeling that if the Lord would forgive him, he could believe Sommer would recover. He waited a moment before putting the poem on the bed and then walked out of her room heading into the hopeless, black night. He had no other thought beyond getting out of the hospital.

He had just stepped into the corridor when he heard his name. In a moment of disbelief, his heart began to race. He had been the only visitor in the room.

Sommer's unmistakable voice asked, "Michael, why did you leave me?"

Michael's mind screamed, "THIS CAN'T BE!"

"Michael, come here."

Did he hear Sommer's voice or was he hallucinating? Did he imagine hearing her voice because his mind was so deflated and shocked and not capable of discerning real from ghostly? Holding to the door for support, a weak, scared man took one step in the room. Sommer was propped up in bed. A minute before, her comatose body was pale and lifeless. She again beckoned him to come to her. He scuffed his shoes on the floor, taking small steps. He could do no better. His legs were ready to collapse but finally reached the bed. Sommer's face was flushed with a relaxed radiance he had not seen before. She squeezed his hand with surprising strength.

Many church members had come in to visit. They were concerned but respectively stayed just minutes offering condolences and pledging to continue praying for a full recovery. Sommer's Pastor, Paul, came every morning and evening, praying and attempting to encourage her mother, aunt, cousin, and Michael with words of hope. After the first day, Michael did not like the pastor. He had decided the accident was entirely his fault, and he was being punished by not ever being able to hold his love again. The pastor stayed upbeat saying God could do anything, including restoring Sommer to the healthy person she was before the accident. He mentioned often that prayer is direct communication with God and one should pray believing God, will hear requests and will answer. Michael once believed that but wavered when he decided he was to blame for this bad thing. But when he had kissed her cheek, he now knew the warm feeling was God's assurance that his prayer was being answered while his unfaithfulness to Sommer was forgiven.

"Michael my dear, I just saw Jesus. I was looking at Him when you kissed me. He was standing at the foot of the bed. Did you see Him?"

Her radiance seemed to overflow on to him. More tears slipped from both of their eyes as a renewed bonding drew their hearts to experience a level of peacefulness neither had known before.

"No my dear, but I could feel His presence when I kissed you."

Sommer responded with the sweetest smile. Everything was so grand and glorious—so extraordinary—so beautiful.

"His eyes, Michael, were so full of love. He didn't speak a word. His message was in His eyes. In an instant, I knew He touched my body, and I knew you would always be by my side."

Dear Reader: If you have ever felt the presence of Jesus in your mind and heart, you know what was happening to Sommer and Michael—a peace which passeth all understanding—

(Ref. Philippians 4:7)

The commotion was no small thing when the nurses and doctors discovered that Sommer was fully conscious and coherent. She wanted to leave but had to stay overnight for observation. She was released at 9 a.m. on Sunday morning.

Chapter Eighteen

Pastor Paul was the only one at church who knew Sommer had been miraculously healed. He visited her room late Saturday night, and in his words, he "Had a shoutin' fit—" They talked about what had happened and decided not to tell the church members until tomorrow morning. Pastor Paul had trouble driving home—tears of joy blurred his vision.

Members and visitors assembled in the Beulah Ann Baptist Church not knowing a special blessing would warm their hearts this cold December Sabbath morning.

Sunday school classes, praying, announcements and singing all took place as usual. There was no variance in any of the worship service format until Pastor Paul stepped behind the pulpit. He began with thanking the church for praying for Miss Sommer Rose. He then asked the congregation if they believed miracles still happen today. There was some head bobbing, some hand waving, and some amen's. Then, with deeper reverence, he asked if the ones who prayed for Miss Rose actually believed God would bring her out of the coma. Then he quickly added, "And restore her to live again and be a testimony to the power of prayer?

By the response it appeared the congregation generally believed in miracles but was not sure about a specific incident such as Sommer being miraculously healed. After an undetected signal from Pastor Paul, Sommer Renée Rose walked down the center aisle to stand in front of her brothers and sisters in Christ. By the pastor's request she was wearing a white dress. By her design she was holding a multicolored bouquet. The visual and spiritual effects exceeded Pastor Paul's intended, current-day proof of what God can do if people pray believing.

Many people would later declare (some may say swear) they saw a halo about Sommer's shining face. There was no question in anyone's mind that her naturally beautiful face did in fact shine with brilliance like an angel might look. And furthermore, one might assume she had just gathered a bouquet from God's Heavenly garden.

There was no sudden eruption of emotions (with one exception) or a stampede to touch and/or embrace the person God awoke from her deep sleep. The prayer believers were the first to come forward. On the fence believers followed. Then God's sweet spirit infused the remaining ones initialing a charge to the front as cattle pressing to a water hole. Holy water was certainly available in this place today. One woman had been shouting since Sommer turned to face a group of stunned and mystified Sunday worshipers.

Tears and more tears flowed in thankful abundance. Sommer had no makeup to smear and streak from the tears cascading down her soap clean face. With a backdrop of the blush on her cheeks from the swelling thankfulness in her heart, reflected light on her tears enhanced the brightness of her face so much that some decided an angel was in their midst.

166

A small older lady hugged the angel and then looked up (Sommer was five feet, nine inches tall) and said, "I believed and knew you would be well again. I knew, I knew." The reality of touching an answered prayer was such a poignant expression of God's love and concern for His own that she required assistance back to her seat.

The teenage youth group meeting in an adjacent building was summoned to witness and praise the glory of God. Nursery minders and children's church leaders meeting in the basement alternately joined the celebration of God's victory over death.

Need it be mentioned that Pastor Paul did not preach a sermon this joyous Sunday morning? Many songs were sang during the time Sommer was standing, praising the sovereignty of God. After the last sincere encirclement of arms around an angel in their midst, Sommer spoke for five minutes about seeing Jesus. She related about her contemptible attitude toward the man she was to marry. She told them that love turned to hate when he stepped over the line one time. The crowd before her knew she had been legally brain dead and recovered but didn't know this part of her personal life. She went on to tell them that after seeing Jesus, her outlook on life completely changed.

"He had already forgiven all my sins and then gave me another chance to live. So how could I not forgive the man I plan to marry? I guess I hated this man so much that Jesus had to make a special appearance to show me how much He loved me and that He wanted me to forgive the man I love."

Michael was one of four first time visitors. He had sat proud as a peacock knowing the angel up front was to be his wife. They had a joyous reunion last night at the hospital.

Two visitors were a middle aged couple. They had held back until after Sommer's testimony. As they slowly moved forward through the happy throng milling around the altar, the lady's crying increased until she had to sit on the front pew to stabilize. They then stood before Sommer and did not touch or embrace her. She smiled at them with the same sweetness that had greeted the nearly 200 people before them. The lady's composure was soon stable enough to speak.

"Could we meet today and pray together? My daughter has been missing for two years. She is now sixteen."

Sommer's perpetual smile faded as she looked in the lady's sad eyes.

In a divinely driven move, Sommer leaned forward and tightly embraced a hurting mother as a peaceful and tranquil feeling flashed through her entire body. It was the same sensation as when she saw Jesus. Sommer withdrew her arms and the mother would have fallen had her husband not been by her side. Pastor Paul was close and heard the mother's request and apparently sensed a spiritual transfer from Sommer to the mother.

He whooped and pranced between the piano and organ and shouted repeatedly, "Thank you, Jesus!" Others became (more) excited because he rarely shouted. When he settled down enough to make a sentence, he told the mother her daughter had started home two minutes ago. He then asked the mother to stand beside Miss Sommer Rose. He told the congregation this mother has a daughter that's been missing for two years. He said she believed her child would return home if Sommer Rose would pray with her.

He whooped again and declared, "The daughter is on her way home this minute. I sensed the power of Jesus move from Sommer to this believing mother. I tell you folks—it's a done deal. Can someone say Amen?"

When the two first time visitors came back to earth, they joined Beulah Ann Baptist church. Many came to the altar to rededicate their life to a fuller service with Christ. The fourth first time visitor was an unsaved man. He had not been in a church, except for three funerals, in forty-five years. He left a saved man. After accepting Jesus as his personal Savior, he said he would have come sooner if he had known Christians had such a happy time in church.

Paul called for Michael to come and stand beside his fiancé. He then said, as he looked at Michael, "This fine young girl got permission directly from Jesus that it was okay to marry you."

Just before closing, an eighty-five year old woman stated that she had been in this church all her life and had never been in a more spirit filled service.

A Pastor, brimming over with the glorious splendor of God's love, announced there would not be a benediction.

"Let's not close this spirit filled service. Shake a hand and hug a neck—see you tonight."

Sommer and Michael returned to the Sunday night service. They were also at the church the following Saturday at 1 p.m. to be married.

 *The End*

Epilogue

The wedding list that Sommer couldn't get right last June was incredibly easy this time. Family members from both sides were contacted by phone, and it was announced as an open church wedding. The church was packed, including a certain thankful sixteen year old girl. The following reception was unadorned but was the best attended and most enjoyed ever at the Beulah Ann Baptist church.

The best laid plans can often change. Michael realized his once elaborate wedding plan with snobbish guests would have been a big mistake. Sommer's simple plan with her church family seemed to make them more married.

Honeymoon plans can also change. A happy, tearful couple, confident their marriage was sanctioned by Jesus, left the church at five thirty for the four hour drive to Serendip.

The newlyweds daily thank the Lord for their many blessings. They are active in a small church—both are Sunday school teachers. They have been returning to Beulah Ann for the annual homecoming, and Sommer is still the horseshoe pitching champ. At least once a year, a group of Beulah Anners visit Serendip. Often, a family will drop in for a short time on their way to Gatlinburg and Dollywood.

Oh yes. twins, a boy and a girl, were born in 2005.

The talked about trip to England (second honeymoon) during July 2004 was beyond their expectations. But that's another story.

ABOUT THE AUTHOR

Harry Beckett is a retired Engineer living in Barboursville, WV with his wife, Betty. Harry dreamed of writing a novel during his career of technical writing and his dream came true in 2002 when his first book was published. This book is his fifth, with more planned during his retirement.

www.ingramcontent.com/pod-product-compliance
Lightning Source LLC
Chambersburg PA
CBHW050746250626
47155CB00005B/1947